JESSIE'S HEART SUDDENLY HAMMERED AGAINST HER BREAST.

Something moved—something right behind the window! Jessie choked off a cry and went to her knees. Kneeling, she drew the long robe about her thighs, then fled in a crouch to the parlor. Quickly she turned the gaslight out. The room fell into darkness. Without looking back, she moved toward the hall. Her only thought was to get out fast . . .

Jessie grasped the knob and turned it. The door held firm. She tried again, panic welling up inside her.

In the smallest part of a second she saw the thing coming toward her—a blur, a shadow, a form as silent as smoke. Jessie cried out as cold pain sliced at her throat . . .

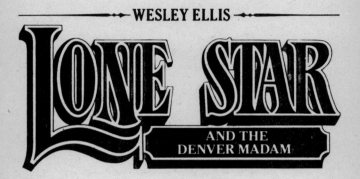

WESLEY ELLIS

LONE STAR

AND THE DENVER MADAM

A JOVE BOOK

LONE STAR AND THE DENVER MADAM

A Jove Book/published by arrangement with
the author

PRINTING HISTORY
Jove edition/August 1983

ISBN: 0-515-07112-9

Jove books are published by The Berkley Publishing Group,
200 Madison Avenue, New York, N.Y. 10016. The words
"A JOVE BOOK" and the "J" with sunburst are trademarks
belonging to Jove Publications, Inc.

PRINTED IN THE UNITED STATES OF AMERICA

LONE STAR
AND THE DENVER MADAM

★

Chapter 1

Even in the elegant marble lobby of the Windsor, Ki looked as if he belonged. His blue-gray tweeds were well cut, his cotton twill shirt was winter-blue, and a plain shoestring tie was knotted neatly at his throat.

Still, he felt uncomfortably confined, like a cat in a fine gilt cage. He and Jessie had rushed north from the Starbuck ranch, making the best connections they could out of Texas. They'd arrived that morning just at dawn, and though Ki had enjoyed a long and luxurious bath, he'd put the travel-worn clothes back on with only a brushing. They itched and smelled of soot. He longed for faded denims and his old vest and shirt. Not exactly the right attire for the occasion, he thought glumly, but a hell of a lot more comfortable.

The newly completed hotel was touted as "Denver's Pride, the Finest Hostelry in the West." Ki thought it more than lived up to its billing. Five stories high, the sandstone and gray rock structure was filled with diamond-dust mirrors, hand-carved

European furniture, and enough red velvet to start a dozen good brothels. Crystal chandeliers lit a forest of potted palms. Smoke from good cigars blended with fine Paris perfume and the pleasant smell of money.

As Ki waited, a circle of men stopped to talk nearby. They were portly, middle-aged gents with well-trimmed beards. Their clothes were of English cut, and all of them wore fashionable beaver hats and silk shirts. Their boots were highly polished, and heavy gold watch chains draped across their bellies.

Ki took them in with a glance and promptly forgot them. His gaze was focused intently on the girl. She was tall and rangy, not too far from an even six feet. Her green gown clung to her figure like a glove. Ki followed the dress with his eyes, tracing the smooth fabric up incredibly long legs to the swell of pert little breasts. One long hand held a furled parasol trimmed with white lace; the other was hooked loosely in her escort's arm. Ki guessed she was half the man's age, likely less than that. Nineteen, twenty at the most. For a moment he thought she might be his daughter, then quickly dismissed the idea. Properly trained daughters did *not* squirm up against their daddies like big, sleepy cats.

As if she read his thoughts, the girl turned her head just slightly and gave him a look. Whiskey-colored eyes swallowed him up, from his head to his Wellington boots. She studied his raven's-wing hair, the sharp planes of his cheek, and the line of his mouth. It was the eyes, though, that caught her glance and held it. His eyes were the mark of his Japanese mother, tilted slightly at the corners. The pupils were dark and intense, close to gunpowder black.

"I don't know you, do I?" she asked softly.

"Not yet, you don't," said Ki.

The girl gave a throaty little laugh. "Lord, we'll have to do something about *that*, now won't we?"

"It would certainly be my pleasure."

"Mmmmm, mine too, I bet." One brow rose to meet a tangle of black curls. "Would tonight be too soon for you?"

Before Ki could answer, the heavyset man on her arm turned and shot him a steely look. "Come along," he said sharply, "we're late, Amanda!"

2

"Yes, Charlie," she purred, and the whiskey-colored eyes winked mischievously at Ki.

With a deep sigh of regret, he watched her cross the lobby until the firm and shapely bottom disappeared. Whoever she was, he wouldn't likely see her again. If "Charlie" had any sense, he'd keep a girl like that in a cage.

"Enjoying the sights of Denver, I see."

Ki jerked around, and the color rose to his cheeks. "Yes, well, I was—"

Jessica Starbuck laughed. "I *know* what you were doing, you don't have to explain. She's a very pretty girl. Are you about ready to get going?"

Ki nodded and stifled a yawn. "What I'm ready for is two days' sleep."

"Nonsense," scoffed Jessie. She grabbed his arm and guided him briskly across the lobby. "A samurai doesn't *need* any sleep. You told me so yourself."

"True," Ki admitted, "but it's the American half that's tired. Unfortunately, they are very closely attached."

A uniformed doorman saw them coming, stepped quickly aside, and opened the ornate portals of the Windsor. Instantly, Jessie and Ki were swept up in the busy traffic of Larimer Street. Carriages, wagons, and men on horseback vied for space on the dusty way. Glancing in both directions, Ki could see the red brick facades and striped awnings of assay offices, drugstores, gambling dens, and saloons. Denver was growing fast and feeling its oats. Gold, and then silver, had turned a sleepy little settlement into the finest city in the West.

Miners, cattlemen, railroaders, and vagrants hurried by, but Ki noted that none were too busy to give Jessie an appreciative eye. Even in a city well known for its beautiful women, Jessica Starbuck was worth a second look. Neither faded denims nor the more formal jacket and skirt she now wore could hide the lush lines of her figure or the beauty of her face. Strawberry-blond hair tumbled freely past her shoulders, framing startling green eyes, a straight, aristocratic nose, and lips that always seemed about to smile. In the bright summer sun her skin was a smooth honey-gold. By the softer light of evening it would turn to fresh cream, the copper in her hair would fade to amber,

3

and her eyes would turn a darker, more sensuous shade of emerald. She was an angel in lace when the right mood struck her, an imp in old demins the moment after. It was a quality that drew men to her, or set them back on their heels.

Jessie and Ki ran the last few steps across the street, reaching the stone sidewalk seconds before a wagon from the Tivoli-Union brewery could run them down. Jessie glared at the driver and turned to Ki.

"Guess it's about ten," she said thoughtfully. "I'll drop by the U.S. marshal's office while you find the paper, all right? We can meet back here for lunch."

"Fine," Ki replied, then asked, "Whatever happened to breakfast?"

"Huh?" Jessie brought a finger to her chin. "Oh, Lord, we forgot, didn't we?" She laid a hand on his arm, and Ki saw a shadow touch her face. "I'm sorry, Ki . . . I'm not thinking real straight, am I? I just can't get Lynnie off my mind. If she's still alive somewhere, she's—she's mixed up with *them*. And if that's true . . ."

Ki shook his head. "If she's here," he said gently, "we'll find her, Jessie. I'll see you at noon or a little after. Say hello to Marshal Long."

His words caught Jessie off guard. "Well, of course, he might not even *be* there," she said quickly. "Probably out on a case somewhere." She glanced at Ki, but he was squinting at something of interest in the sky. "All right," she said. "Noon it is, then. Maybe we'll go to Delmonico's and get fat!" She blew him a quick kiss and scurried off down Larimer.

Ki watched her go until she disappeared past the busy corner of Eighteenth Street, then turned and walked north. The streets were lined with third-rate hotels and gambling houses. A sign touted Zang's Beer at a nickel a glass. Next door, a walkup hotel offered rooms for twenty cents. Ki walked on toward Twentieth. Abruptly he found himself in the heart of Denver's red-light district. There were a few opulent brothels like Jennie Rogers's place, and Mattie Silk's "House of Mirrors." He knew, though, that most of Holladay Street's whores worked in dreary one-room cribs hardly wider than a bed. On a good Saturday night, a girl made enough to buy laudanum and whiskey through

4

the week—unless a customer cut her throat to save a dollar.

Two girls lounging before a door looked up as he passed, saw that he wasn't interested, and let their smiles fade. Ki walked another block, decided he'd taken a wrong turn, and started back the way he'd come.

The man quickly dropped his eyes to the fly-specked window, intently studying the dusty collection of used harness and saddles. Ki came instantly alert. He'd caught the stranger's glance for only a second, but that was enough. The man had been following him, Ki was absolutely certain. He walked straight ahead, showing no concern at all. When he passed, the man was still looking at the harness.

Ki's head didn't move, but his eyes flicked quickly about the street, briefly touching every man and woman in his sight. In a moment he found what he wanted. The second member of the pack was a down-on-his-luck miner, a stooped old fellow nursing a bottle. Only Ki knew he wasn't drunk at all, and certainly not old. He walked too straight, his body didn't sag, and there was too much spring in his step.

That accounted for two of them, then. There'd almost certainly be a third. Ki couldn't spot him, but he was confident the third man would be the best of the lot—the one he'd have to stop.

Without missing a step, Ki turned north toward Blake. The moment he was out of sight he broke into a run, then cut down an alley to Twenty-first Street. He stopped then, and stood perfectly still and listened. After a moment, a grin spread the corners of his mouth. Two pairs of boots were running rapidly toward him. The third man was somewhere else—too smart to make a noise.

Ki hesitated another few seconds, turned south again, crossed Eighteenth, and turned up Wazee Street. Denver suddenly looked different, and he knew where he was. This part of Wazee was called Hop Alley. Chinese laborers had built the railroads, then stayed on in Denver when there was no more work to be had.

Ki paused and listened again. The men were right behind him, better at their job than he'd imagined. There was a narrow alley to his left. He slipped quickly inside and scurried for the street beyond. The muddy stretch of ground was strewn with garbage. A stack of old lumber and rusty tools was piled hap-

5

hazardly against a wall, along with crates of empty bottles. Ki slipped on rotten cabbage, caught himself, and stayed on his feet. When he looked up again, the man was watching him from the far end of the alley. He was heavy, built low to the ground. A broad grin parted his dark and grizzled features. He gripped a ten-inch blade in his hand, and he no longer looked like a miner.

Whirling about, Ki knew what he'd find. The man who liked harness was coming up behind him. His weapon was a short, wicked-looking section of pipe. The striking end was thicker than the other, where he'd wrapped it tightly with lead.

Ki nodded. He understood their thinking. Guns brought the law, and they wanted none of that. Their weapons would kill him quickly, with no noise. Good. He'd fight them the way they wanted. The man with the knife would be the easier of the two; Ki would take him first, after he found himself a weapon.

Hesitating only a moment, Ki drew a deep breath and broke into a run, screaming as loudly as he could and waving his arms. The man with the club stepped back a pace and stared, certain his prey had gone berserk. Ki came at him, yelling like a demon. The man bent in a crouch, gripping the heavy weapon.

Suddenly, Ki leaped high in the air, twisted his body, and kicked out savagely with one leg. The stack of old lumber and dusty bottles exploded. Ki's assailant cursed and stumbled back under a barrage of shattered wood and broken glass. Ki bent quickly, found what he wanted, and turned to face the man with the knife. The other hadn't moved. He stood at the end of the alley, his long blade catching the glare of the sun. For a moment he stared curiously at Ki, saw what he had in his hand, and laughed out loud. His intended prey was either crazy or suicidal. The "weapon" he'd chosen was no more than a broken hoe, a slender staff of wood with the metal edge gone. The man with the knife was delighted. Holding the weapon at his side, he came at Ki in a crouch, moving fast and low.

Ki let him come. Suddenly he was no longer in a Denver back alley. His enemy's face vanished, and became the familiar features of his old *sensei*. The staff he held was a *bo;* its use had taken Ki ten long years of aches and bruises to perfect,

6

and even then, old Hirata could still set him flat on his back with little effort...

The man with the knife suddenly lunged, the blade slicing straight for Ki's belly. Ki stepped aside. The *bo* was a blur in his hands. It whipped the air in a circle and slapped the man hard in the small of his back. The man howled and went sprawling, then caught himself and turned, eyes black with anger. Ki held the *bo* out before him, gripping the staff with both hands. This time the other circled him with caution. He knew, now, that this curious weapon was something more than a piece of wood. It could hit, and it could *hurt*. He feinted to the left, stabbing the air at Ki's shoulder. Ki blocked him quickly. The man stepped back, tossed the blade to his other hand, and came in fast. Ki brought one end of the *bo* around hard and opened a ruddy cheek, then thrust the other end solidly between the man's legs.

The man paled, dropped the knife, and gripped his groin. Ki finished him quickly with blows to the shoulder, head, and belly. The man folded like a sack. Ki felt more than heard the man with the pipe coming up behind him. He let the *bo* slide through his hands, gripped one end like a bat, and whipped it around fast. The man with the club cried out and backed off. Ki didn't let him get his bearings. He drove in relentlessly, the *bo* moving like a whisper. It cracked the attacker's ribs and broke his wrist. Three punishing slaps turned his features to red meat. Without a sound, he collapsed a few feet from his companion.

Ki backed off, bent his knees, and turned in a circle, searching the high brick walls on either side. The third man was there, the one he'd never seen. Ki could sense him, almost feel his dark eyes watching. For the small part of a second, a terrible, unreasoning fear reached out and turned him to ice. Ki accepted it calmly, with no shame at all. He knew what it was: Death had touched him lightly, brushed him with its wings, then vanished abruptly.

He stood up straight and let out a breath. The presence was no longer there. He glanced at the two men. One was stirring, wiping blood from his mouth. The other lay still. He would live, but he wouldn't hold his club for quite a while. Ki knew he could make them talk; in a matter of seconds they'd eagerly tell him everything they knew. But they would know nothing at all, nothing of any value. If he could—

Ki spun around fast, slashing the *bo* through the air like a saber. The girl stood frozen, eyes as big as silver dollars, hands pressed flat against her cheeks.

"J-Jesus Christ," she blurted, "I never saw anything like that in my life. What the hell *are* you, mister!"

★

Chapter 2

Ki searched the street and the alley. Except for himself and the girl, the area was deserted. "Miss," he said evenly, "I think it would be a good idea to get out of here, if it's all the same to you."

She glanced at the pair on the ground. "You're not going to wait for the police?"

"Later, perhaps," said Ki. "Not now." She gave him a narrow look. "I have reasons," he told her. "I'm sure you wouldn't be interested."

The girl's face brightened. "Well, now don't be too sure about that." Ki started hurriedly down the street, and she fell in step beside him. "What *were* you doing down here, anyway? It's not exactly the best part of Denver to go for a stroll."

"I was looking for something. I took a wrong turn."

"Looking for what?"

"You ask an awful lot of questions," Ki said irritably.

"I know," she said cheerily. "I'm supposed to. That's my job."

Ki stopped and frowned. "What is? Watching street fights in Hop Alley?"

"Yeah, sometimes. I'm a reporter. For the *Rocky Mountain News.*"

Ki stared, then broke into a laugh. The girl fumed, and shook a small fist in his face. "You think that's funny, do you? Well, let me tell *you* something, mister. I am damn good at what I do—as good as any man and better than most! So don't go giving me any stuff about a woman doing a—"

"Hold on a minute," Ki stopped her. "I didn't mean anything of the sort. It's just that the paper was where I was going, before I got waylaid back there."

The girl blinked and bit her lip. "It was?"

"Yes. I just went the wrong way."

"Why were you going to the *News?*"

"I need help. Information the paper might have."

"Oh? Information on what?"

He caught the almost-too-casual manner of her question and stopped short. "Why do I get the idea I shouldn't tell you anything at all?"

She gave him an impish grin, and Ki took a good look at her for the first time. She was a short, slightly built girl with almost childlike features. Her hair was a tangle of dull, mousy curls that likely hadn't seen a brush in a week. Her nose turned up at the end, and there was a smudge of black ink on her chin. The clothes she wore were drab and ill-fitting, and a good five years out of fashion. A broad-brimmed hat was jammed on her head, the crown topped by a broken yellow feather. Ki was certain there was an attractive young lady hiding somewhere inside this badly wrapped package; he was also sure she'd hit him in the teeth if he even hinted she might be pretty.

The girl's lively brown eyes caught him and held him. "If you're saying what I think you're saying, you're wrong," she said sharply. "Unless you're a—a *criminal* or something, whatever you tell me won't go any further than me. A good story's one thing, and I'll get one from you if you've got it. But I'm real strong on ethics, and you can take that to the bank. Listen, you're *not,* are you?"

"Not what?"

"A—criminal felon."

"No." Ki grinned. "I'm the victim of the crime. Remember?"

"Huh! You could've fooled me." She gestured with her chin over her shoulder. "Those fellows back there might argue the point. What kind of stuff was that, anyway? The business with the stick?"

Ki walked quickly down the street toward Cherry Creek. Satisfied that no one was following, he doubled back to the heart of town.

"The stick is called a *bo*," he told her. "Fighting with a staff is *bojutsu*. A man who knows the *bo* well can defeat a practiced swordsman, and even—" Ki stopped abruptly, and looked at the girl in alarm. She'd pulled out the stub of a pencil and was frantically scribbling away on a scrap of paper.

"Uh, sorry," she grinned sheepishly. "I get kind of carried away." She dropped the pencil in her purse and stuck out her hand. "I'm Annie McCullough, and I promise no more notes, right? And the *News* is that way, friend, not straight ahead. Mister, you need a bell on your collar, you know?"

The small room was hot and dusty. A narrow, dirty window cast a weak beam of light over rows of wooden files piled high with yellowed paper. Ki sat across from the girl over a small table and told her his story. He sensed he could trust Annie McCullough, and knew she could help him cut corners—especially if she smelled a good story in the making.

Annie promised faithfully not to use anything he told her, unless Ki gave his permission. The first time he mentioned the Starbuck name, she nearly came out of her chair, but somehow managed to sit still and listen.

"Jessie Starbuck and Lynnette Harley were friends," Ki explained. "Really more like sisters. They grew up together in San Francisco, and even when the Starbucks moved to Texas, Jessie and Lynnie went off to school together. They kept in close touch after that, writing letters back and forth. Until Lynnie stopped writing."

Ki paused and squinted at the ceiling. "Two years ago, Jessie got a clipping in the mail from a friend in New York. It was a story from the *London Illustrated Times,* and told how Lynnette Harley had been killed in a hotel fire. The story went

11

into pretty lurid detail about the number of deaths, and the way everyone had died."

"Lord," sighed Annie, "how awful for Miss Starbuck!"

"It was," Ki said. "Jessie got over it, of course, but she could never really forget." He stopped and made a mark on the dusty table. "That was two years ago. Four *days* ago, Jessie got a short note from here in Denver, in Lynnie's handwriting. It said simply, 'Aunt Emma is sick. Lynnie.'"

Annie McCullough sat up straight. "But if she's dead—"

"Exactly. Jessie is *certain* the note is in Lynnie's hand. And there was no one else who could have known about Aunt Emma. It was the name of a favorite doll they shared when they were children."

Annie thought a long moment. "And that's all? No address, nothing?"

"Nothing. Just the Denver postmark."

"And the message. 'Aunt Emma is sick.' From that, Miss Starbuck thinks this Lynnie may be alive and in some kind of trouble, right? I can see that, but—" She paused and raised a brow at Ki. "There's a part of this you're not telling me, isn't there?"

"Yes, there is," he admitted. "I'd have to leave that up to Jessie. I work for her, and she's a friend. I have her trust, Annie, but there are certain things I'd rather let her tell you herself."

"All right." Annie nodded reluctantly. "I understand that. Finding out where Lynnie is, though—that's not going to be too easy. You know that, don't you? Denver's a pretty big place."

"I can be of some help there," said Ki. Reaching into his jacket, he brought out a small envelope, opened it, and handed the photograph inside over to Annie. "Lynnie had this made while she was still writing to Jessie, and sent her a copy."

Annie took the picture, glanced at it quickly, then rose from her chair to look at it in the light of the window. "I don't know, she's a very pretty girl, but there are a lot of—oh, my God, it *can't* be!" Ki saw her features go suddenly slack.

"What? What is it?" He came out of his chair and went to her side.

Annie didn't answer. She tore off her hat and tossed it on

12

the table, then got up and went to a nearby file cabinet. Opening one of the drawers, she said, "If I'm right, I'm afraid we won't have to search very far. I'm almost sure I've seen that face before, and the girl's name wasn't Lynnette Harley."

She pulled out a file folder and opened it, then leafed quickly through its contents as she walked back to the table.

"Aha! There, I was right!"

She drew from the folder a newspaper clipping illustrated with an engraving that depicted a formally dressed man and woman. Attached to the clipping with a wire clip was the photograph from which the engraving had been copied for publication. The story was headed, "A Tragic Death on the Eve of Their Wedding. Lovely Bride-to-Be Expires in Her Sleep."

In the engraving, the faces of the couple were ambiguous, as was usual in newspaper pictures of this type. But the photograph—mounted on card stock—was clear. Even though the girl in the photograph had light blond hair, whereas the hair of the girl in Ki's picture was dark, it was obvious that both pictures were of the same woman. The caption on the engraving identified the girl as "Marie D'Avenant, famed French beauty." Ki recognized the man without reading further.

He was California's U.S. Senator Marcus Hall. His name had been in the news for several years. He was from a wealthy and powerful family, a man who'd made a reputation for himself by rooting out corruption in his state, and in the nation's capital as well.

"It has to be Lynnie," said Ki. "Lord, now I've got to show Jessie the *second* death notice on her friend." He glanced at the rest of the story, then looked up at Annie. "What's this supposed to mean—'expired in her sleep'? What did she die of, do you know?"

Annie let out a breath. "We didn't print it, but the doctor said her heart simply—stopped."

Ki raised an eyebrow. "At what? Twenty-two, twenty-three?" He glanced at the date on the clipping. No wonder it hadn't taken Annie long to find the story; it was only ten days old. The story was dated the twelfth. The death had occurred on the evening of the eleventh. Today was the twenty-second. The letter had taken a week to reach Texas . . .

With a sudden chill, Ki remembered the postmark date on Lynnie's note.

"She mailed the note on the eleventh," he told Annie. "The same day she died."

Jessie sank back in the sofa in the hotel lobby and stared at the picture. She'd shed tears for Lynnie two years before, and couldn't bring herself to cry anymore. "I guess I ought to be shocked or something," she said softly. "Only I'm not surprised at all, Ki. I didn't think she was really alive. I guess I was . . . right and wrong at the same time."

Annie sat on the edge of her chair and looked miserable. "I'm very sorry, Miss Starbuck. I wish I could've dug up some better news."

"Call me Jessie, and it's not your fault." She reached out and squeezed Annie's hand. "I'm grateful for your help. Really." Jessie looked at Ki, her green eyes troubled. "What was she doing here?" she asked. "Obviously she had some reason for taking another name, not letting anyone know she was alive. But *why*, though? I can't believe she was mixed up with . . . with *them*, Ki."

"I think we have to," Ki said gently. "You know she didn't die in her sleep, Jessie. And if she didn't, that means they killed her." He paused and looked at his hands. "There's something else, too."

"Lord, now what?"

Ki told her quickly about the fight, that he was certain the men weren't street thugs after an easy dollar. For the moment he kept his thoughts about the third man to himself.

Jessie let out a breath. "They know, then. They already know we're here. Ki, that may be why they killed her. Maybe they knew she sent the letter. Maybe they——" She made herself say the words. "Maybe they made her talk before she died. God, poor Lynnie!"

"Look," Annie said suddenly, "I know I'm a stranger here, but would either of you mind telling me who *they* are? I don't have the slightest idea what you're talking about!"

Jessie and Ki looked startled; for a moment, they'd forgotten the girl was there. Jessie exchanged a look with Ki, and Ki nodded.

"I'm afraid the whole story would take all day, Annie, but I can give you part of it in a very few words. We know Lynnie was murdered, and we know exactly who's responsible. Here. Look at this." She drew a small scrap of cloth from her jacket and laid it in Annie's hand. "Lynnie sent that in her letter. That's why Ki and I left Texas the same day."

Annie McCullough turned the small piece of cloth over in her fingers. It was the torn corner of a delicate Belgian linen handkerchief. Embroidered into the cloth was a highly stylized crown. Annie looked up, a question in her eyes.

"That symbol is the mark of a powerful European business cartel," explained Jessie. "Ki and I have fought them for a long time. They murdered my father, and they'd very much like to see me dead as well."

Annie McCullough frowned. "And you think they killed your friend, too?"

"No." Jessie shook her head firmly. "I *know* they did, Annie; I don't have the slightest doubt they're behind it. I don't know where Lynnie comes into this, but there's no question now that she was involved."

Annie looked appalled. "My God, Jessie. I've heard of businessmen playing rough—but going around killing people!"

"You can believe it," Jessie said flatly. "This isn't your ordinary brand of businessman, Annie. The cartel is powerful and ruthless. They want the wealth of this country in their pockets, and they'll stop at nothing to get it. Murder, bribery, coercion—nothing matters, as long as they get their way."

Annie moaned and slapped her forehead. "Damn! The biggest story I'll every get my teeth into, and I have to go and promise to keep quiet. Me and my fool ethics!"

Jessie leaned forward and took her hands. "Annie, when we find out what happened to Lynnie, I'll gladly let you out of that promise. You can write whatever you want—if anybody'll print it."

Annie looked puzzled. "Now what's that supposed to mean?"

"Stories about the cartel have a habit of . . . disappearing, before they ever get into print. You don't know what kind of

15

men we're dealing with here. Or just how far they can reach."

Annie's jaw clamped tight and her eyes bored into Jessie's. "Well, I'll tell you one thing sure. No one's ever stopped Annie McCullough from getting a story into print—and no one ever will!"

Jessie insisted that Annie join them for dinner, and Annie quickly accepted. Then, when she learned they'd be dining that evening at Charpiot's "Delmonico of the West," just down the street from the Windsor, the girl went weak in the knees. She'd never even been *inside* the place before, had nothing to wear, and didn't think she could manage it at all. Jessie said she wouldn't hear of her not coming, and Annie paled and fled the hotel.

When she arrived at the restaurant, Ki checked twice to make sure it was Annie. Somewhere she'd begged or borrowed a gown that clung to her body like paint. The girl had luscious curves and hollows he'd never dreamed she possessed. The mouse-brown hair wasn't mousy anymore. It swept up the back of her neck in silken coils, setting off the fresh, clean glow of her skin. Jessie saw the bewilderment in Ki's eyes, and raised a menu to hide her grin.

The dinner lasted until well after ten. Annie and Jessie chattered away like schoolgirls, and Ki sat back and smiled like a cat. Even without the envious glances of every man in the room, he knew he was dining with two of the loveliest women in Denver.

Annie did her best to impress Ki and Jessie with her "Delmonico" manners. Only once did the real Annie McCullough show through. After lavish courses of fish, chops, roast duck, vegetables, and fine cheeses—as well as musty bottles of exquisite French burgundy and chablis—she caught a quick glimpse of the check. It came to nearly eight dollars, a figure she could scarcely believe.

"My God," she blurted aloud, "no wonder none of those bastards ever took me in here. I've *got* to get some high-class men!"

Jessie and Ki laughed, and Annie turned as red as a beet.

* * *

Ki had no idea how hard the wine had hit Annie until they got outside on the street. She wobbled and nearly fell, then suddenly burst into song. Ki saw Jessie to a carriage, then held Annie up until another came along.

Once inside the closed cab, Annie came quickly into his arms. Soft lips searched him out; the rapid pulse of her breath was as hot as fire against his throat. Surprised, Ki returned her kisses, meeting the girl's hunger with his own. The instant he thrust past her lips with his tongue, Annie gave a sharp little cry and went rigid. Uncontrollable spasms shook her body; her arms and legs thrashed wildly about, beating at the sides of the carriage.

Startled, Ki backed off, certain that the girl had suffered some terrible seizure. Annie's brown eyes went wide. She reached out desperately, drawing him back in her arms.

"Oh, Lord," she said wondrously, "you know how *good* that was? I never felt anything like it before!"

Ki blinked in the dark. "Annie, are you talking about . . . what I think you're talking about?"

Her eyes tried to focus on his. "You like it all right, Ki? It was all right, wasn't it?"

"Uh, yes. Just fine, Annie . . ."

Annie giggled, reached past him, and flung her skirts up high. In the dim light from the street he caught the quick flash of her legs, a tantalizing glimpse of silky down between her thighs.

"Didn't wear any petticoats or stockings . . . now, how'd I forget that!" Annie threw back her head and laughed.

"Annie," Ki said calmly, "you've been drinking quite a bit, and I don't think you're used to it. You might be doing something you wouldn't be doing if you—"

"You mean I'm drunk? An' maybe you're seducing poor ol' Annie? You're damn right you are, friend!"

"Uh, what I think we'd better do—"

"—is do it *again*," Annie finished. "Now, Ki—*please!*" Her legs scissored around him, pulling him hard against her. Ki wasn't certain what 'again' meant to Annie, but the swelling of his crotch told him he was on the right track. He was glad the driver, on his perch outside the enclosed cab, couldn't see

17

them. Annie ground herself against him, thrashing her head from side to side. The ache was growing steadily in his trousers. Ki eased her back to get at his buttons. Annie didn't notice that he was gone. Her back curved in a bow, and her lush little mound beat steadily at the air.

Finally his swelling member was free. He found the smooth flesh of her thighs and brought her to him. As his hand touched her skin, Annie exploded again, gave a blissful sigh of pleasure, and went limp. Ki stared, then moaned under his breath. In seconds, she was snoring gently away. He reached out and grasped her before she slid to the floor.

"Mister," called the driver, "everything all right back there?"

"No, damn it, it's not!" Ki blurted. "Just keep driving!"

★

Chapter 3

Ki made his way painfully up the stairs of the Windsor, cursing the luck that had placed him in a fifth-floor suite. At the moment he would have traded the spacious quarters for a flophouse cot. His hapless encounter with Annie had left him bent nearly double. The walk back helped, but his loins were still heavy with a dull and nauseous ache that made every step an effort. Better that, he thought glumly, than a bouncy ride in a carriage . . .

Jessie had made a tiny mark on her door, a signal they sometimes used. It told him she was safely in her room across the hall. Wearily he turned the big key in the lock and opened his door. The parlor was as he'd left it, the gaslights turned down low. He locked the door securely, turned—and came instantly alert. Something was wrong. Different. His dark eyes flicked about the room. A chair was moved slightly. One of the fine imported rugs was slightly askew. More than that, the suite was heavy with new and unfamiliar smells. A slight, spicy scent, not unpleasant at all. It mingled with the odor of tobacco and something else he couldn't define.

Pulling off his coat, he let it drop to the floor, then bent to slip out of his Wellington boots. The bedroom door was open a crack. He pushed it back slowly with his foot, pressing his body flat against the wall. The carpet appeared, then the brightly patterned wallpaper, the polished brass bed, and the tawny flesh of the girl . . .

Ki stared, and stepped into the room. The girl stirred, stretching long arms over her head. The motion pulled the sheet past her shoulders, baring her breasts.

"You're late, you know," she said sleepily, peering at Ki from under a tumble of dark hair. "God, tonight means *tonight*—not the next day. What time is it?"

"Ah—close to twelve, I think," Ki said absently. "Look—what are you doing in here?" The words sounded ridiculous as soon as he said them. The girl laughed and sat up, showing him the impish, whiskey-colored eyes he remembered from the morning.

"If I have to tell you, we are in big trouble, friend." She swept hair out of her eyes. "I don't, though, do I? I never make mistakes about men. Oh, I'm Amanda. And you're who, or what?"

Before Ki could answer, she tossed the sheet aside and pranced naked across the room. In spite of the aching in his groin, the sight of her sent a surge of blood through his veins. Her body was long and sleek, a sensuous mix of lean, velvety hollows and curves. She walked without a sound, like a big, lazy animal on the prowl. Her incredibly long legs seemed to go on forever, then swell to creamy thighs. Ki caught a glimpse of secret places, a neat little nest between her legs. She stopped then, and turned to show him her plushy rounded bottom and the curve of her back. Her clothes were draped over a lacquered Chinese screen; she stretched on the balls of her feet, found the pocket of her gown, and came up with a delicate, slim cheroot. Twisting on the trim line of her legs, she faced him again, a hand braced jauntily on her hip. She struck a match to the cheroot and blew a thin plume of smoke in his direction.

"Want one?" she asked him. "They're fine Havanas. I have them made special. Do you object to women smoking?"

"Not many do, but I don't object at all." Ki grinned and let

20

his eyes trail boldly over her body. "To tell the truth, I wasn't really looking at your cheroot."

Amanda laughed. "Didn't figure you were. I can tell, because that *lovely* cigar of yours is about to rip right through your trousers. Lord, it looks delicious—and I haven't even *seen* it yet! Guess I better correct that problem right now."

Before Ki could answer, the tall girl was on her knees, her hands working quickly at the buttons of his fly. His erection sprang free, and Amanda's amber eyes went wide. "My, if that isn't fine. Just about the most—" Ki flinched and jerked away as her hands found his balls. Amanda looked puzzled, then a knowing grin creased the corners of her lips. "Uh-oh, don't tell me. I *thought* you looked all bent up and bothered. What happened—one of the girls down at Bella Bernard's tease you up and leave you hanging? No, wait—not your style at all. A man like you wouldn't—" Her eyes sparkled with delight. *"Not Jessica Starbuck herself!* I know you two are traveling together . . ."

Her words trailed off as Ki's eyes went hard. "I work for Jessie, and she is a friend. That's *all,* Amanda."

Amanda shrugged. "Whatever you say. Seems kind of peculiar, two good-looking people like you. Anyway, it doesn't much matter, does it? Someone's got you all hot and bothered and left you hurting. Going to have to do something about that before you and I can have any fun."

"Just what did you have in mind?"

"Don't you worry about that." She cradled his erection in her hand and stroked him gently. "Amanda's going to fix you up fine, all right?"

Crushing out her cheroot in a porcelain bowl, she closed her eyes and gently touched the tip of his member with her lips. The ache in Ki's groin came alive, then quickly subsided as she slid his shaft gently into her mouth. From the first moment she touched him, Ki knew the girl was a master of her craft. He was schooled in the arts of love, and took pride in his ability to prolong the lovemaking process. Amanda, though, clearly knew every trick in the book. If Ki closed his eyes, he could imagine he was in the experienced hands of a Japanese geisha. Where a young American girl had learned and practiced a courtesan's ways, he couldn't guess.

21

At some other time, he would have tried to match her skills, play the game that would take him up to lofty heights. Now, though, he didn't fight her at all. He welcomed the warmth of her mouth, the quick little tongue that fluttered delightfully over his shaft. He could feel the heat stirring deep within him. It sang through every nerve, swelled like a fire in his loins. Amanda knew exactly what she was doing. Amber eyes grinned through the dark veil of her hair. She looked right at him, let her lips part slightly till he could hardly feel her at all. Ki hung suspended on the high crest of pleasure, only a touch from joyous release. She held him there a long, agonizing moment, eyes flashing with mischief. Then, with a kiss as light as a whisper, she trailed the tip of her tongue from the base of his shaft to the tip...

The storm within him exploded. Amanda took him fully into her mouth, wrapped her arms about his waist, and raked his back. Ki filled her with his warmth, one thunderous surge after another, until he was certain he'd never stop. Still, Amanda refused to let him go. He was empty, drained, limp with sated pleasure. And at that moment, Amanda touched him deftly with her tongue once more...

"My *God!*" Ki moaned, nearly jerking out of the chair in surprise. The orgasm shot like a bolt into his groin, bringing a new release even greater than the first.

Ki lay back and let out a sigh. "I don't know what you did to me, woman. I think maybe I'm dying."

"Not yet, you're not!" Amanda sprang lightly to her feet and put her hands on her hips. "I finished what some other girl started," she pouted. "Now it's *my* turn, friend." She caught Ki's look of alarm, threw back her head, and laughed. "Hey, you can rest a couple of minutes. There's no big hurry."

"Fine," Ki said dryly. "A couple of minutes would help."

Amanda danced past him and moved naked to the far side of the bed. Ki heard an unfamiliar sound, turned, and saw her wheeling a small cart across the floor. The cart held a large bucket of ice and a chilled bottle of champagne.

"I ordered up a Moët Chandon. Hope you like good champagne."

Ki burst into laughter, reached out, and pulled the girl off her feet. Amanda cried out, sprawling in his lap in a tangle of arms and legs. He kissed her soundly, then held her back and grinned.

"Who *are* you, anyway?"

The girl cocked her head. "I'm Amanda. I already told you that."

"Yes, but Amanda *who?*"

"Who cares?" she said lightly. "I'm here, aren't I?"

"*I* care," said Ki. "I have no complaints at all, Amanda, and I can't think of anyone else I'd rather have perched on my lap. But I do like to know who I'm loving."

Amanda grinned and kissed him on the nose. "All right. I'm Amanda van Rijn. My husband's name is Charles van Rijn, and I live in a big house on Capitol Hill and I'll be nineteen in April. Satisfied?"

Ki sat up straight, nearly spilling the girl to the floor. "You're married to *that* Van Rijn?"

Amanda sighed and made a face. "Don't worry about good old Charlie. He doesn't have any idea where I am. Never does, thank God." She sprang out of his lap and began wrestling with the bright foil neck of the champagne bottle. In a moment the cork popped free with a small explosion. Amanda lifted the bottle to her mouth and took a deep swallow. Bright rivulets ran down her cheeks and over the high peaks of her breasts. She passed the bottle to Ki with a grin. Drinking wasn't one of his habits, but the cold, tangy liquid tasted good. Setting the bottle down, he glanced uneasily over his shoulder. It wouldn't have surprised him at all to see the portly, outraged figure of Charles van Rijn bursting into the room, with half of Denver's police force at his heels. Even as far away as Texas, Ki had heard of "good old Charlie." Along with men like Tabor, Sheedy, Campion, and Nathaniel Hill, Van Rijn had built Denver from a collection of shacks along the river. Bedding the lovely young Amanda wouldn't likely earn Ki points with the city fathers.

Amanda guessed his thoughts. Clutching the champagne, she plopped down in his lap again and turned him to face her. "You aren't afraid of Charlie, are you? You don't have to be, you know."

Ki looked pained. "I'm not exactly afraid, Amanda. I'd be kind of stupid not to be concerned, though, now wouldn't I?"

"You want me to go?"

"Of course not." He grinned. "I'm not stupid, just crazy."

Amanda laughed and twined her arms around his neck. "You know, you never did tell me your name."

"You never gave me much time. My name is Ki."

"Ki what?"

"Just Ki. It's the only name I have."

"I never knew anyone with only one name."

She'd been in his lap only a short moment, but the warmth of all that honey-sweet flesh was almost more than Ki could bear. He kicked his trousers free, lifted her in his arms, and carried her across the room to lay her gently on the bed.

"And I've never known anyone with legs as long as yours," he told her. "Lord, Amanda—they do go on forever!"

"Do you like my body? Really, Ki?" Black hair tumbled loosely over the satin pillow. She gave him a lazy look from under a thick fringe of lashes.

"I like your body just fine," he said. "You are one of the loveliest girls I've ever seen. Truly, Amanda." He slipped off his shirt and joined her on the bed. She slid easily into his arms.

"I liked the way *you* looked right off," she whispered. "You were hard and tall. And your eyes—" She leaned up on one arm and ran a finger lightly over his brow. "I just love the way they turn up at the corners."

"I'm half Japanese," he explained. "The eyes are from my mother."

"And where'd you get *this?*" she teased him, sliding her hand past his belly.

"Ah, I grew that myself."

"Well, it grew just fine, I'll tell you that!"

He was rock-hard already, just from being near her, but the expert touch of her hands made him swell even more. "The way you touched me when you loved me just now—you have a rare talent for pleasing a man. Where on earth did you—"

Amanda suddenly stiffened and pulled away. "Where did I learn to *do* it so damn good?" she said sharply. "Well, I'm not one of your 'soiled doves' from Holladay Street, if that's what you mean!"

Ki was taken aback at her anger. He reached over and

24

brought her to him. "I meant nothing of the kind," he said firmly. "Amanda, there is no shame in a man and a woman making love. And there is nothing wrong with knowing how to give pleasure to your partner. I didn't mean to pry, or offend you in any way."

She looked at him, and her amber eyes softened. "No, I don't guess you did, did you? Ki, you want to know what I am, then I'll tell you."

Ki kissed her: "I know what you are. You are a wonderfully exciting woman."

"I'm rich too," she said shortly, "and I'm sure not sorry about that!"

"There's no reason why you should be."

She reached up and took his cheeks between her hands. "I've got a good idea you don't come from any real grand beginnings yourself, and that sure doesn't make you any less of a man. Want to hear the honest-to-God truth about Amanda? I grew up outside Denver, in a dugout cabin on the Platte. My ma washed clothes and my pa sold bad beef and deer meat to the miners till they caught him and beat him to death. I was fifteen when he died. Ma kept working till she dropped—to keep me out of one of those cribs on Holladay Street. I was growing up fast—men were following me around like dogs after a bitch. If Charlie hadn't found me, I'd likely be dead or worn to a nub." She shook her head and laughed out loud. "I wouldn't let him touch me unless he married me. Can you believe that? I was sixteen and a half. He couldn't stand *not* to, so he did. Told all his friends I was a rich orphan from a real fine family in Chicago."

Amanda's voice sank to a whisper. "That old man was the first I ever had, Ki. I haven't forgotten that, and I wouldn't do anything that'd shame him in front of his friends. But now and then I've got to have a man who can handle me. Either that or go crazy. And to answer your question, no one taught me a thing about loving. Guess I've got a natural knack, 'cause I sure do like it a lot!"

Ki was silent for a long moment. "I'm sorry," he said finally. "I had no business asking."

"I wouldn't have said a thing if I hadn't wanted to. I think you know that." She reached down and grasped him again, and her whiskey-colored eyes went hard. "Mister, if you don't put that in me real soon, I'm going right out of my mind. You understand what I'm saying?"

Ki gave her a lopsided grin. "Yes, I understand, Amanda."

"And you can wipe that fool smile off your face right now, 'cause I know exactly what you're up to. You haven't touched my breasts at all, or put your hand between my legs. You're just waiting and watching me squirm!"

"You're right. And it's not easy, either."

Amanda's eyes flashed. "Oh, it's not, huh? Well, how do you think *I* feel when you—oh, Lord!"

Ki slid his hands past the curve of her throat to the swell of her breasts. He let his fingers trail lazily over the pale, creamy flesh, marveling at the way the pert little mounds were both delightfully firm and satiny soft. Amanda moaned and closed her eyes as he kneaded the pliant skin, moving his fingers in ever smaller circles toward the dimpled rosettes.

"Kiss them, Ki—*please!*" Her words were fierce explosions against his throat. "Don't tease me any longer!"

"I've hardly gotten started," said Ki.

Amanda groaned and gritted her teeth. With the tips of his fingers, Ki gently flipped the soft coral bud of her nipple. Amanda gasped and jerked beneath him. Instantly her nipples tightened to firm buttons. He stroked the silken tips, watched them turn from pink to dusty scarlet, then bent to take the sweet little points into his mouth. Amanda gave a ragged cry of joy, tangled her hands in his hair, and ground his face against her breasts. The musky taste of her flesh sent a sharp surge of excitement through his veins. He sucked the spicy nipples past his lips again and again, until her breasts were flushed with color. Amanda thrashed wildly beneath him, pressing the length of her body against his erection. Ki ran his hands down the curves of her back, grasped her waist, and drew her to him. With a soft squeal of laughter, Amanda kicked her long legs in the air, boldly displaying her treasures to his eyes.

Ki rose quickly to his knees, relishing the incredibly lovely sight of the young girl before him. Amanda arched her back in a slender bow, pressed her toes against the sheet, and brought her bottom off the bed, her knees spread wide, opening the lush heart of her pleasure like a flower. Ki's pulse quickened.

It was a trick only a girl with Amanda's body could perform. Her lean and rangy frame had equipped her with extraordinary muscular control. As he watched, supple tendons in her legs went taut, forming tender hollows along her thighs. He was certain she could stretch no further, but Amanda wasn't finished. Her heels came together until the plane of her legs from one knee to the other was nearly flat. The effect swelled Ki's already rigid member. The girl's tight belly went flat, thrusting her feathery mound upward in a proud and jaunty arc.

"Do you like it?" she asked softly, the words almost slurring in her throat. "I *want* you to see me, Ki, everything I've got. Do you know what that does to me? Do you?"

"I know what it does to *me*," Ki said dryly.

Amanda laughed. "Maybe if I . . . did this a little, just kind of twitched some for you . . ." Resting her hips on the cushion of her heels, she moved her pelvis in a slow and lazy circle. The downy nest teased him, begged him to sample its joys. He could feel the heat of her body, almost taste the sweet honey between her thighs. Still, he forced himself not to move, not to reach out and take her. He knew the waiting pleased her, heightened her excitement.

Moving closer to her, he brushed the tip of his shaft lightly against her. Amanda bit her lip and tossed her head from side to side. Her hands snaked quickly between her legs to grasp his hardness. Desperately she fought to bring him closer, to thrust him into her warmth. Her fist encircled him gently, caressing him with the moisture from deep within her. Ki closed his eyes and let out a breath. He was determined to hold her off, to take their pleasure as far as he could.

Amanda, though, was having none of that. He'd forgotten the girl's skills, how she'd taken him where she wanted to only moments before. Practiced fingers danced lightly over his member, swelling his hunger nearly to bursting. Ki fought for control and nearly lost it. Amanda gave a wicked little laugh, and ground herself against him.

Ki laughed with her, brought his throbbing member to bear, and thrust himself deeply inside her. Amanda screamed with pleasure. Her legs scissored tightly about him, trembling against his back. Now all the chains were broken. Ki gave her everything he had, holding nothing back. He pounded her relentlessly, slamming himself against her again and again. Amanda shouted her delight, giving as good as she got.

Ki knew exactly what she wanted—the hard, savage side of love, where the giving and the taking were one and the same. He wrapped his arms around her, felt the softness of her breasts flattened against him, filled her mouth with thirsty kisses...

Once more he sensed the swelling deep inside him, the fierce, churning heat that threatened to rise up and engulf him. Amanda knew his hunger and writhed against him, thrusting him deeper inside her with the pressure of her legs. Together they soared to great heights, grasped each other tightly, then burst into a white-hot ball of fire. For a moment the mingled pain and pleasure were almost too much to bear. Amanda cried out, matching Ki's deeper groans of delight. Their eyes met and smiled—his as dark as night, hers all smoke and copper...

"Listen," she said softly, "you'll let me know, won't you?"

"Huh?" Ki gave her a puzzled look. "Let you know what, Amanda?"

"You know. When you're ready to get started. We were thinking about some real fancy loving, remember?"

Ki's jaw fell. Amanda tried to keep a straight face, but Ki's expression set her laughing. It was contagious, and they laughed for a long time before settling down once again to the business at hand...

★

Chapter 4

Jessie quickly shed her clothes, leaving them tossed about the room wherever they fell. Leaving a gaslight burning low in the parlor, she sank back exhausted on the bed. The luxury of a soft feather mattress brought a sigh of relief to her lips. The shocking news of Lynnie and the long subsequent trip from Texas had taken their toll. What she needed most now was a good night's sleep. In the morning she could find out whether the man Lynnie had planned to marry was still in Denver; Annie McCullough could likely give her some help with that.

Lord, she wondered suddenly, *could a man like Hall possibly be involved with the cartel? If he isn't, was it Lynnie herself? God, I won't let myself believe that!*

Jessie turned over irritably and pounded her pillow. Too many thoughts were spinning through her head, and sleep wouldn't come. Why would her friend pretend to die—then show up somewhere else to die again? What was she doing in Denver? *What did Lynnie know that got her killed?*

Jessie moaned and slipped out of bed. Padding wearily to

the window, she pulled back the curtains and stared out at the darkened city. It was well past eleven, and most of Denver was buttoned up tight. A few yellow lights winked here and there—gaslights along the main street, at the depot, in some gambling halls and saloons.

With a yawn, she let the curtains fall and tumbled back into bed. Light from the room beyond cast a soft lemon shadow across her breasts, down the hollow of her belly and the length of her legs. She was naked except for a thin gold chain about her throat, and a bright red garter around her thigh. The chain was a gift from her mother; the garter she'd fashioned herself. Tucked behind its frills was a small, ivory-handled derringer, the grips engraved with the Circle Star brand. She'd worn the little weapon so long, it seemed a part of her now.

Is this the way it has to be? Will I have to wear a pistol all my life, awake or asleep?

She'd asked herself the question more than once, and knew there was no ready answer. She had inherited her father's vast holdings, as well as the curse that went with them—the seemingly endless fight against a circle of faceless men. It had started before she was born, when Alex Starbuck had carved a great business empire for himself, built on trade with the newly opened ports of Japan. There he'd run afoul of the shadowy European cabal, a group of powerful men bent on making their own fortunes in the Orient. Not content with a mere share of this lucrative market, they wanted it all for themselves, and were determined to destroy all who stood in their way.

Alex Starbuck was a strong and stubborn man. He'd earned what was his, and he meant to keep it. The cartel struck out at the Starbuck interests, and Jessie's father struck back. Ships were burned and cargoes destroyed, but the bitter fight didn't end there. Soon, death became a part of the game. Jessie's mother fell victim to the cartel's assassins, then Alex Starbuck himself. When they'd gunned him down on his own ranch in Texas, Jessie took up the fight.

It goes on and on, she thought wearily. *Lord, there's likely no end to it, ever!*

Lying alone in her bed, Jessie thought suddenly of Custis Long. The image he brought to mind sent a quick wave of pleasure through her body, and put a mischievous grin on her face. She'd known many men in her life, but the man known as Longarm held a very special place in her heart. She was disappointed he wasn't in Denver, but not overly surprised. His job kept him constantly on the go.

That afternoon, she'd spent a good hour with Longarm's boss, U.S. Marshal Billy Vail. Vail had tried to be helpful, but he could shed no light on Lynnette Harley. Jessie reminded herself to let him know they'd learned who Lynnie really was. That information put the matter in a different light. Vail could use his sources to—

Jessie stopped, suddenly alert as the sound intruded on her senses. It was a faint, almost imperceptible scratching, like some tiny animal scurrying about. *Probably just what it is*, she decided. Even a first-class hotel like the Windsor would have a few mice.

She lay back, mashing her pillow to a comfortable mound. Almost at once, the sound came again. This time she sat up straight, a chill at the base of her neck.

"The hell it is," she said softly. *"That's* no mouse, Jessie Starbuck!"

Crawling quickly out of bed, she drew a thin robe about her shoulders, plucked the derringer out of her garter, and slipped it into her pocket. Moving to the wall, she stood still and listened. Whatever the sound was, it was close, so close she could— *God, what if it's right here, right here in the room!* She shook the thought aside and took a deep, calming breath. Light from the parlor laid a path across the floor. She let her eyes touch every wall in the room. The washstand. A table. An overstuffed chair. The dark armoire in the corner, and then the entry to the parlor. Past that, the two large windows overlooking the street. The windows were half open, the filmy curtains puffed slightly from the breeze...

Her heart suddenly hammered against her breast. *Something moved—something right behind the window!* Jessie shrank back. It couldn't be, it was impossible. Her room was five stories above the ground. No one could be out there—*no* one!

At that instant, the shadow slid across the window like a wraith. Jessie choked off a cry and went to her knees. Kneeling on the floor, she drew the long robe about her thighs, then fled in a crouch to the parlor. Quickly she turned the gaslight out.

The room fell into darkness. Without looking back, she moved toward the door to the hall. Her only thought was to get out fast. The hall would be lit, and she'd be safe. Ki was right across the way. One quick knock, and he'd be wide awake and at her side.

Jessie grasped the knob and turned it. The door held firm. She tried again, panic welling up inside her. Suddenly she knew what was wrong. She'd locked the door and taken out the key. God, where had she *put* the damn thing! Glancing over her shoulder, she was certain she heard a sound. A soft squealing noise, then a tight little click. *Like someone opening a window . . .*

Desperately, she felt around in the dark. There was a table by the door. She remembered then, and jerked the drawer open. Her fingers touched the key lying inside. Gripping it hard to keep from shaking, she fumbled for the keyhole, found it, slipped the key in quickly, and turned. The lock gave a satisfying click. Jessie gripped the knob—then froze in her tracks and jerked around.

In the smallest part of a second she saw the thing coming toward her—a blur, a shadow, a form as silent as smoke. Something left the darkness, whispered past her cheek, and buried itself in the wall. Jessie dropped to the floor and brought the derringer up fast. The weapon roared twice, bouncing white fire off the walls. The shadow stumbled back and raised its arms in a motion much too fast to follow. Jessie cried out as cold pain sliced her throat. The dark form paused; she felt its eyes right on her. Suddenly the door splintered behind her, spilling harsh light into the room. Ki gave a blood-chilling yell, landed in a low fighting crouch, and disappeared.

Jessie didn't move. It seemed like forever before Ki padded out of the bedroom.

"Are you all right?" he asked anxiously. "I only got a glimpse of him, but— My God, get away from there, Jessie!" Before she could move, Ki leaped forward and pulled her roughly to her feet. "Get some light in here—quickly!"

Jessie obeyed, found a box of matches, and lit the gaslight on the far wall. When she turned, Ki was kneeling on the floor, staring intently at the thing buried in the molding by the door.

"Oh, Christ!" Jessie shrank back, drawing the thin robe

32

about her shoulders. There were three of them—small, murderous-looking hatchets: one beside the door, where she'd heard the intruder and turned; two closer to the floor, where she'd crouched and fired the pistol. The two lower down were less than seven inches apart—just room enough to frame her head. Jessie spotted something on the floor, looked closer, and felt her stomach turn over. It was a long strand of copper hair, sliced neatly by the weapon's sharp blade.

Ki wrenched one of the hatchets out of the wall. In spite of his strength, the cords in his shoulders strained with the effort. The hatchet was crescent-shaped, like a three-quarter moon. The shaft and the blade were fashioned from one piece of steel. Ki hefted the weapon in his hand and made a noise in his throat.

"It's nicely balanced. A very fine weapon."

"I'm real glad you think so," Jessie said shakily. "Ki, that creature had to *climb* the damn building to get in here. He nearly—"

"Jessie, it's all right. He's gone." Reaching into his pocket, he brought out a bandanna and dabbed it lightly at her throat. Jessie backed off in surprise, her face suddenly pale. "It just nicked you," he said calmly. "Sit down and I'll get you some brandy."

Jessie sank into a chair, her knees suddenly weak. *That thing could have taken off my head*, she thought numbly.

Ki heard frightened, cautious voices in the hall, footsteps pounding up the stairs. He turned and peered out the shattered door, then back to Jessie. She hadn't even noticed that the gauzy robe had slipped off her shoulder, nearly baring the swell of her breast. Ki looked quickly away. "You'd better get dressed," he said evenly. "Looks like we're in for a lot of company real soon . . ."

Jessie couldn't remember a longer night. It seemed as if every guest in the hotel had found his way to the fifth floor, as well as more than a few wanderers off the street. Someone told the local papers that Jessica Starbuck had been murdered in her sleep; in moments the police had a near riot on their hands. One of the steel hatchets disappeared; pieces of the ruined door were carried off as souvenirs.

When the police finally left, Jessie fled to Ki's room and

sank wearily on his bed. She was exhausted, but not too tired to notice the bucket of melted ice and the empty champagne bottle. More than that, there was the spicy hint of perfume on his pillow. *Definitely not Annie McCullough*, she thought wearily, and drifted off to sleep.

Ki lay on a couch in his parlor, but didn't close his eyes. Someone had tried to take Jessie's life, and he didn't intend to let them reach her again.

"I just want you to know I didn't have a *thing* to do with that, Jessie. Honest to God, I didn't. I've got no idea how they found out, but *I* didn't tell them!"

Annie sat on the edge of her chair, looking miserable. The table in Ki's parlor was set with a lavish breakfast. Annie refused even coffee, and wouldn't look Ki in the eye. The feast was courtesy of the Windsor's manager, who politely suggested they'd be more "comfortable" there than in the dining room downstairs.

"I know you didn't," Jessie assured the girl. "*I* told them, Annie. Part of the story, at least. The people who want me dead are obviously well aware of why I'm in town. I saw no reason why the law shouldn't have that information too."

Annie looked relieved, then angry. The *Rocky Mountain News* lay on the chair beside her. The headlines read:

HEIRESS ATTACKED!
HATCHET-WIELDING MADMAN SOUGHT

JESSICA STARBUCK SAYS, "SENATOR'S BRIDE WAS MY CHILDHOOD FRIEND!"

The story gave a garbled account of the attack, and an even more inaccurate version of Jessie's revelations about Lynnette Harley.

"Lord, Jessie, it must've been just *awful!*" said Annie. She strained forward in her chair, her wide eyes locked on the small piece of tape at Jessie's throat. "You didn't get a good look at him at all?"

"No. Just a shadow. A quick look when I fired at him. It was all too fast, Annie."

34

"The paper says you hit him—that there was a lot of blood on the carpet."

Jessie smiled wearily. "There was a *drop* or two—not bucketsful, I'm afraid."

"Jessie hit him," put in Ki. "But not enough to put him out of action. He threw those last two hatchets *after* she fired her pistol."

Annie shuddered and clasped her hands nervously in her lap.

"I think you can help us, if you will," said Jessie. "I'd like to talk to Senator Hall. Do you know if he stayed on in Denver after Lynnie's death?"

"Oh, he's still here," Annie said eagerly. "Only I don't imagine he's going to be too happy over that story about Miss Harley, you know?"

"Senator Hall will simply have to face the truth, along with the rest of us," Jessie said firmly. "Where is he staying, Annie, do you know?"

"Oh, sorry. He's a houseguest of Elaina Culbertson's. You know, *that* Culbertson? Henry Culbertson was a friend of Senator Hall's father. Mrs. Culbertson's got a big ranch north of town."

Jessie nodded thoughtfully. She knew little about Elaina Culbertson, but her husband was almost a legend in the West. Like Goodnight and Chisum, he'd made his money bringing cattle north to market. Culbertson, though, hadn't stopped there. He was a shrewd businessman with an uncanny talent for being in the right place at the right time. The money he made in cattle went into Denver real estate, banking, railroading, and gold and silver mines. Jessie remembered that he'd been dead now a good five years, shot in an argument over cards. He'd left his widow, Elaina, more money that she could spend in a dozen lifetimes. The lavish parties she gave every season couldn't begin to make a dent in the Culbertson fortune.

"Guess we'll have to take a ride out to that ranch," Jessie told Ki. "Marcus Hall might be able to tell us something about Lynnie."

"He knew her as Marie D'Avenant, though," said Ki. "It looks as if Lynnie fooled him, along with everyone else."

"Maybe," Jessie agreed, "but I cannot believe a man and a

35

woman could get close enough to marrying without finding out *something* about each other, even if—"

Jessie paused as someone knocked lightly on the door. Ki rose quickly, asked who was there, then opened the door a crack and closed it. "It was a boy from downstairs," he said. "This came for you."

He handed the cream-colored envelope to Jessie; she opened it and took out the folded card inside. She glanced at it a moment, then sighed and shook her head.

"What is it?" asked Ki. "Something wrong?"

"No," she said slowly, "just kind of peculiar, considering what we've been talking about, Ki. It's an invitation. Mrs. Elaina Culbertson's asked me to supper."

★

Chapter 5

The vast Culbertson ranch lay to the northwest of Denver, on land that swelled gently toward the Front Range of the Rockies. As the carriage took them along the dusty road, Jessie studied the scenery with a practiced and critical eye. Whoever was running the place knew what they were doing. The cattle looked good, and all the hands were keeping busy. Close to the house, they passed a crew moving out to ride fence. A wagon followed the riders, its bed piled high with rolls of barbed wire and lengths of cedar poles. The riders waved, and Jessie waved back.

"You haven't said a word in the last five miles," Jessie told Ki. "Thinking about last night?"

"Yes," Ki said soberly. "Last night, and before that, Jessie." He turned to face her, his dark eyes troubled. "I felt that man's presence in your room; I sensed his power, and the darkness of his mind. He had the smell of *ninja* about him."

Jessie raised an eyebrow at that, and Ki quickly shook his

37

head. "No, I don't mean he's Japanese. I mean he has the *ninja* soul. He is a most dangerous man."

"I guess I already knew that."

"Not all of it," said Ki. "I didn't tell you before. He was there when the men attacked me on the street. He could have killed me while I was busy with the others. He could have, but he didn't."

Jessie felt a chill touch her spine. "Why, though? Why would he hesitate, Ki?"

"I don't know. Testing me, perhaps. Seeing what I could do." Tension strained the corners of his mouth. "Do you see what that means? He's telling me he can take me when he wishes. That he can get by me and reach you."

"No." Jessie shook her head firmly. "I don't believe that, Ki."

"He nearly did last night," Ki said soberly. "He climbed the side of that building, five stories high. He was gone before I—" He stopped, and looked right at her. "Jessie, I know you won't do it, but I've got to ask anyway. I want you to leave Denver now. Get back to town and get the first train out. If you won't drop this business with Lynnie, then let *me* stay—"

"Ki..." Jessie laid one hand on his arm. "I love you for what you're trying to do. I *can't* leave. You know that."

"I know that you are a very stubborn woman," he said shortly.

Jessie forced a laugh. "Yes, I guess you do, don't you, if anyone does. I'm Alex Starbuck's daughter—and Sarah's too. Not much I can do to change."

Ki didn't answer, but Jessie could almost read his thoughts. He would lay down his life to keep her from harm, but there was always a chance he might fail. Jessie had long ago learned to accept that possibility. She knew, though, that it was something Ki could never accept.

Elaina Culbertson surprised her. She must have been close to sixty, but the lady actually looked ten years younger. Time had pared her figure and set the firm lines of her mouth a little tighter; still, she was a classically beautiful woman, with sparkling blue eyes and a bright, engaging smile.

"I am *so* glad you could come," she said warmly, laying a white-gloved hand on Jessie's arm. *"Please* don't think badly of Denver, my dear. Heavens, what a ghastly experience— you must have been petrified, I'm sure. I met your father once in Austin. Or was it San Antonio? I simply cannot keep them straight. A *very* handsome man."

Jessie thanked her graciously and introduced Ki. Elaina Culbertson hesitated only a second, then muttered a greeting in Ki's direction. Jessie hid a smile behind her hand. She was certain it was the first time a person who was even *half* Oriental had come through the front door.

Jessie grinned at Ki. "Come on, I won't let anyone eat you."

"Just keep me away from the laundry and the garden," Ki said grimly. "That lady'll put me to work on the spot."

Jessie laughed, started to turn, and then stopped. Elaina Culbertson spoke to another guest, then moved across the hall. For the first time, Jessie realized she was lame. Her right leg was nearly useless, she pulled herself along with the aid of a silver-handled cane. Jessie's heart went out to the woman. When she walked, she was a completely different person. Her face became a mask, and the pain showed clearly in her eyes.

Jessie and Ki passed through the corner of a large parlor, a room filled with Mexican rugs and dark, heavy furniture. The house was built in the sprawling Spanish style, and the parlor gave way to a walled courtyard dominated by a splashing stone fountain. Colorful lanterns had been strung overhead, and costumed musicians in wide sombreros wandered about. Jessie guessed there were twenty or so couples on hand, and she was certain they were the cream of Denver society.

"If it's all the same to you," said Ki, "I'll wander over and see if there's anything to eat. I'm half starved from the ride."

"Huh!" Jessie gave him a narrow look. "What you mean is, you don't want to meet a bunch of people, right?"

"I want to meet them about as much as they want to meet me. You're the notorious guest. The one they came to see."

"Don't remind me," Jessie said tightly. "They're trying not to stare, but I feel like the main act in the circus. It's probably exactly why Mrs. Culbertson invited me. Go on," she laughed, pushing Ki away. "If you find any food, you can bring me some too."

Ki walked off, a look of vast relief on his face. Jessie decided she couldn't stand in one spot all evening, and walked out on the patio toward the fountain. Almost at once a stocky, broad-shouldered man with a touch of silver in his hair edged through the crowd and stalked toward her, a tall young blond on his arm. Jessie was struck by the girl's breathtaking beauty. She was sensuous and full-figured, almost bigger than life. In another time and place, she could pass for a Viking queen.

"Miss Starbuck? I'm Lane Forsman, senator from Colorado," beamed the man. "I'd like you to meet my wife, Barbara."

"We are so glad to have you here," said Barbara. "What happened was just terrible. Is there anything we can do?"

"Thank you," said Jessie. "Not a thing, really. But I appreciate your asking." Barbara Forsman's voice was as smooth as warm honey. Her eyes, though, told Jessie a different story. They were as cold and brittle as blue northern ice.

"While you're here," said the senator, "you got to come up to *our* ranch, ma'am. Got a place a little to the west. Good air, and more game than you ever saw."

"Oh, yes," purred Barbara. "You simply must, Miss Starbuck."

"Please. Jessie's just fine."

"Jessie . . . of course." Barbara arched a regal brow of disapproval, then covered the gesture quickly with a smile. "You must come if you can. We'd *love* it. Truly. Oh—dear Elaina seems to need me. Take care of Jessie, will you, Lane?" She turned then, and glided elegantly through the crowd.

"My pleasure, I'm sure," said Forsman.

"What? I beg your pardon?" Jessie shot him a questioning look.

"I said it'd be my pleasure. Taking care of you, Miss Jessie."

Jessie felt the color rise to her cheeks. There was no mistaking the meaning in Forsman's words, or the look in his eyes. He was grinning from ear to ear, his gaze locked boldly on the swell of her breasts.

"I'm quite sure you don't mean that the way it sounds, Senator."

"Well now, that's where you're dead wrong, little lady." He took a step closer. Jessie smelled the odor of good bourbon

40

on his breath. "I *always* mean what I say."

"Now, really . . ." Jessie forced a smile and backed away.

"You're a very beautiful woman, Jessie. I mean that."

"So's your *wife,* Senator."

Forsman's smile faded. For a moment his eyes blazed with fury. Then, just as quickly, he took a deep breath and shook his head. "You'll have to forgive me, Miss Starbuck. Afraid it's the whiskey talkin', and not me. I'd be grateful if you'd overlook this entirely."

"Yes," Jessie said coolly, "I'll do that."

"No, I mean *really* forgive me. Please." For a moment he looked like a little boy caught in the cookie jar, and Jessie had to laugh.

"All right. You're forgiven. But don't let it happen again."

"Honest, I swear." His ruddy face split in a grin, showing remarkably white teeth. "Can you excuse me a moment? Couple of fellows I got to see. You wait right here now."

Forsman bounded off, shouting out a greeting to a group of men nearby. Jessie watched him, and let the anger she felt show in her eyes. Senator Forsman had handled the whole thing as smoothly as silk; no doubt it was an act he'd practiced and polished over the years. If the lady bites, fine. If she doesn't, hang your head and bring on the charm. The lady forgives you, and likely goes away flattered that a man like Lane Forsman finds her attractive.

Jessie found no fault in a man letting her know his desires. At times she openly welcomed such attention, and let the man know it. Forsman, though, would never approach a woman with such honesty. *Talking* her into bed was part of the game. Jessie suspected it was the part he liked best . . .

Ki balanced a plate of roast beef and potato salad in one hand, a glass of lemonade in the other. He didn't spot Jessie, but figured she was somewhere close. Skirting the crowd, he found a bench where he could put down his food. Just across the way was Elaina Culbertson, holding court from an ornately carved chair. Most of the men and their ladies stopped to chat and moved on. One man, though, never left her side. He was a short, cadaverous fellow dressed in a tight black suit. His skin had a pale, unhealthy cast, as if he never saw the sun. Small, birdlike eyes were lost behind the spectacles perched

41

on his nose. Ki didn't like to drop a man in a slot, but he looked for all the world like the local undertaker.

Suddenly, Ki completely forgot the man in black. The woman crossed the floor toward Elaina Culbertson, turning every man's eye as she passed. The fabric of her tight satin dress flaunted every curve of her body. Pale blond hair swept like a crown to the top of her head, the color a perfect match for the unblemished flesh of her shoulders and breasts. Ki had never seen a woman quite like her. Every feature was perfect, from the full and sensuous lips to the haunting blue eyes. She was a statue come to life, a—

"You so much as *touch* that one, and I'll cut off your hand right at the wrist!"

Ki turned quickly at the sound of the voice over his shoulder. "Amanda! What are *you* doing here?"

Amanda van Rijn grinned at his discomfort and sat her shapely bottom down beside him. "I was invited, silly. You forget, I am a very important lady in this town."

"No, I haven't forgotten that," he said soberly, glancing warily over his shoulder.

"Hey, don't worry about ol' Charlie. He's out in back somewhere, smoking a cigar with Horace Tabor—you know, the one who's putting up our opera house?" Amanda gave a shrill little laugh. "If his wife ever finds out he's fooling around with Baby Doe, Horace'll be singing tenor when that damn place opens, and—oh, *Lord,* Ki, I almost had a stroke when I saw the papers. You're not . . . *hurt* or anything, are you?"

"No," said Ki, "I'm just fine, Amanda."

Amanda suppressed a shudder. "Don't guess I missed it by much, did I?"

"About half an hour. I'm glad you weren't there. We had all the excitement we could handle."

Amanda looked pained. "Lord, you're as right as you can be. I don't think Charlie would've liked that at all. Is it all really true, what they said in the papers about Marie D'Avenant not being Marie at all?"

"It's true, Amanda."

"I don't imagine Marcus Hall's going to like that, Ki. He really loved that girl. An awful lot, I think."

Ki sat up straight. He'd only known this delightful girl in

42

bed; it was hard to keep remembering she was Amanda van Rijn, who probably knew everything worth knowing in Denver.

"Did you ever meet her, Amanda?"

"I didn't really know her very well. But I saw her a lot. We went to the same parties and all."

"Do you know anything about her? Where she came from, what she was doing in Denver?"

"A little, I guess." She bit her lip in thought. "She wasn't here all that long, Ki. She and Marcus Hall fell in love just like that. They were only together a few weeks."

"You don't know where she came from in France?"

"No, not really."

"Did she have any special friends while she was here? Anyone who knew her before she came to America?"

Amanda's eyes brightened. "Oh, yes. Barbara did. That's who she was staying with. They met when Barbara was in France, and got to be friends. She's the one who introduced Marie to Senator Hall."

"Barbara?" Ki looked puzzled. "Barbara who?"

"Barbara Forsman, dear," she said coolly. "You know? The one you had all undressed a minute ago? She's Senator Lane Forsman's wife."

"Oh. That one."

"Yes, that one. And I meant what I said, mister. You keep away from her. *I* saw you first. Which reminds me, I have *got* to have you inside me again soon. God, right *now* would be just fine with me. We could kind of wander off behind the wall there and— Ki! Ki, where on earth are you going? Come back here right now!"

Ki was already gone, dodging past the fountain and toward the house. He'd spotted the heavyset gent moving rapidly through the crowd, a fat cigar puffing angrily in the side of his mouth. Without looking twice, he knew it was "good old Charlie" van Rijn . . .

He was standing with a small group of men when Jessie walked up behind him. He seemed to sense that she was there, and turned to face her, anger already flaring in his eyes.

"Senator Hall," said quietly, "I'm Jessica Starbuck."

"I know who you are," he said coolly. "You have made

43

that perfectly clear to everyone in Denver."

Jessie flushed and brought herself up straight. "I don't want to fight with you, Senator. I didn't come here for that. If you want to be rude, I guess that's your privilege. I came here to talk about Lynnie, because I loved her. For a big part of my life, she was the best friend I had, and I miss her."

Marcus Hall regarded her for a long moment. He was younger than Jessie had imagined, no more than thirty, she was sure. His deeply tanned face and rugged features surprised her; he looked more like a lawman or a rancher than a politician who spent his time indoors.

"You knew *someone,*" he said calmly. "Someone you've mistaken for Marie. But my fiancée was not this other person, Miss Starbuck."

"Someone thinks she was," Jessie said bluntly. "I've got the blood on my neck to prove it."

Hall shook his head. "I'm sorry for the danger you were in last night, believe me. But it had nothing to do with Marie."

"Oh, no. And neither did the note 'Marie' sent me the day she was killed. And neither does this, Senator Hall." She took the picture out of her purse and held it out to him.

"No!" Hall's eyes went wide. He backed away from Jessie as if the picture might scorch him. "I don't need to see that. *It is not Marie.* Do you understand that, damn you! It—is—not—*Marie!*"

Every face on the broad patio turned to stare. Marcus Hall's face went slack. He stared past Jessie as if he didn't see her at all, then turned and staggered back through the crowd.

For some reason she couldn't fathom, Jessie looked to the right just then, and found herself facing Elaina Culbertson. The lady gripped the arm of her chair with bloodless hands. Her features were taut with terror, as if the devil himself had suddenly dropped in uninvited to her party . . .

★

Chapter 6

"It's a pleasure to see you again, Miss Jessie—and you too, Ki," said Marshal Billy Vail. "I'm real sorry Longarm couldn't be here, but you know how it is with that tall drink of water. He does try not to stay around civilized folks any more than he has to—and we try to oblige him."

"I'm sorry too," Jessie said, thinking wistfully, *And that isn't the half of it.* "But it's sure good to see you, Mr. Vail—uh, Billy," she amended, remembering that they were on a first name basis. "You know, you really should drop down and visit us again sometime, under pleasanter circumstances than the last time."

Vail smiled. "I'd surely like to do that," he said, and nodded toward the blizzard of paperwork that, as usual, completely covered his desk. "But those consarned pencil-pushers in Washington keep me busy right here. I can see Longarm's point about civilization, sometimes."

He indicated a newspaper that was lying atop one of the piles of paperwork. "I see you've been pretty busy yourself

45

since the day before yesterday. Quite a brouhaha over at the Windsor. The papers had a lot of fun with it."

"Didn't they, though?" Jessie said wryly. "You can understand why I didn't come back and see you yesterday."

She told him briefly everything that had happened since their last meeting, two days ago. When she had finished, Vail leaned back in his chair and passed a pudgy hand over his bald head. His expression was grim.

"The Prussians and their cartel again, eh?" he said. "They do like to mess around in politics, don't they?"

He remembered the incident that had recently taken him and his deputy, Custis Long, to the town in Texas that had been founded by Jessie's father and named for Jessie's mother, Sarah. The cartel's machinations in that case had led to the deaths of many people, including several of Vail's deputies, and had left Vail himself with a painful memento in the form of a bullet hole in his right side.

Unconsciously, he rubbed at the healed wound as he said, "Don't take me wrong, now. You're always welcome here, and I'll do anything I can to lend you a hand. The thing is, the Denver police get all hot and bothered if I poke my nose in their business." He blew out a breath and scowled at the picture of President Hayes that hung on his office wall. "You can bet your life they know you're up here right now—and what you had for breakfast, besides."

Jessie nodded and glanced at Ki, then back to Billy Vail. He was a heavyset man with a ruddy face and a shiny bald head fringed with gray hair. In the small office he looked like a big, sleepy bear holed up for the winter. His eyes, though, told a different story. Vail was an alert, highly intelligent lawman who knew his business. Very little happened in the state that he didn't hear about by suppertime.

"I understand perfectly," Jessie told him. "If anyone asks, this is strictly a social call. I have nothing against the Denver police—but I do trust you, and I simply can't take a chance on them."

Vail leaned forward on his desk. "You know something I don't?"

"No. And I'm sure they're fine men, for the most part. But

46

you know as well as I do that Denver's run by a handful of powerful men. I don't want my words getting to the wrong people."

Vail nodded and said, "Makes sense. I've been digging up some facts—if you can call them that—since I read the story of the doin's at the Windsor. Wish I could say different, but I don't know any more about Marie D'Avenant than I did about Lynnie when you asked me the other day."

"Well, *I* learned something—or rather, Ki did," Jessie said. "Did you know Barbara Forsman was Lynnie's—or Marie's—close friend? That she met her in France, and introduced her to Senator Hall right here in Denver?"

Vail straightened abruptly. "You're not trying to link Senator Forsman with this business, are you? That's stepping on some pretty big toes."

"I realize that," Jessie replied. "Do you know anything about them?"

"Who, the Forsmans? Hell, he's a United States Senator. I know everything there is to know about him. *And* his wife, and their dogs and their cats. Everybody in Colorado knows the Forsmans."

Jessie's green eyes narrowed. "Billy, you know very well that is *not* what I'm asking."

Vail said nothing, but Jessie knew he understood. Longarm worked for Vail, and he'd been right at Jessie's side during the investigation of her father's murder. For his part, Vail was well aware of the cartel's power, having experienced it firsthand. Jessie had shown him the monogrammed corner of the handkerchief she'd received from Lynnie. Vail hadn't batted an eye, or seemed overly surprised.

"I know what's involved here," he said finally, "and I don't have a doubt in the world your friend was murdered. Or that the same people who did her in sent a killer after you. But I am not about to believe Lane Forsman's mixed up with people like that."

"Someone is," Ki blurted abruptly. "They've tried to kill Jessie once, and you can bet they'll try again!"

Vail looked him straight in the eye. "You are dead right, son, and I know it." He pulled his bulk out of the chair and leaned over his desk. "That's a part of this job I don't like a whole lot. There isn't a hell of a lot I can do—not till I get something solid to go on."

"Like what?" Ki said shortly. "Jessie with an axe in her head?"

"You shouldn't have been that hard on him," said Jessie. "He's right, you know. Even though he's a friend, legally his hands are tied. He can't do a thing until we have real proof."

Ki glared at the passing traffic, then guided Jessie quickly over a curb. "Fine," he snapped, "I'll apologize later. Damn it all, Jessie!"

"I know." She laid a restraining hand on his arm. "I may be crazy, Ki, but I can't get those people out of my mind. I don't care who the Forsmans are, they're tied too close to Lynnie, in too many ways. Besides, I plain don't like 'em. They . . . act like something they're not."

Ki had to grin. "Many of the guests at that party fit that description."

Jessie ignored him. "I wish I'd picked a better place to have a run-in with Marcus Hall," she said wearily. "I'd like to talk to Elaina Culbertson again, but I don't imagine I'm welcome out there now. Honest to God, Ki, you should have seen that lady's face. She was scared out of her wits. She *knows* something, I'm certain of it!"

Ki gripped her arm and led her into the lobby of the Windsor. "When I talk to Annie, I'll ask her how close the old lady is to the Forsmans. She'll know, if anyone does."

Jessie gave him a mischievous little wink. "And if she doesn't, you've got another friend who will."

"Yes, I suppose so . . ." Ki flushed and cleared his throat. "Stay here," he said firmly. "*In* the hotel. All right? If you go up to your room . . ."

"I know. There are plenty of Denver police hanging around."

"Right. So use them, Jessie." He paused, and glanced angrily about the lobby. "Hell, they might as well be doing *something.*"

Ki stopped a young boy with an oversized eyeshade and asked directions. The boy pointed vaguely across the room and hurried on. Ki made his way through a forest of desks and spotted Annie in a corner. She turned, saw him coming, and glared.

"Well, what the hell do *you* want?"

"What's wrong? I stopped to ask you to lunch."

"Oh? Well, you picked a good day for it, friend." She gave a harsh little laugh. "I'm free all day —*and* tomorrow, *and* the day after that."

Ki shook his head. "I don't understand."

"I got fired," she said harshly. "About five minutes ago." Annie's eyes went misty and she gritted her teeth. "Come on, pick up one of these boxes, as long as you're standing around. God, Ki, *please* get me out of here before I start bawling. I couldn't stand that!"

Annie wouldn't speak until they got to her room across town. Once inside, she dropped the belongings from her office desk, broke into tears, and fled the room. In a few moments she was back, her eyes red and swollen.

"Sorry," she said soberly, "guess I had to get that out." She plopped on a couch and stared past him. "It was just like Jessie said, you know? I mean, my boss didn't actually *say* it was because I was hanging around with you two. Hell, he didn't have to. It was written all over his face." She bit her lip and looked at him. "I sort of believed what you and Jessie said about this cartel business, Ki. Now I know it's true. And I didn't even write a thing—I was just there!"

"I'm very sorry, Annie."

"You know what makes me madder than anything? My boss and his boss, clear on up to the owner, likely have no idea just where the *suggestion* to fire Annie McCullough came from. It was just a—just a favor for a friend of a friend!"

"Ah." Ki nodded. "Now you're beginning to understand how the cartel works. Look, I'm sure Jessie will help. She has a great many friends."

Annie laughed at that. "Funny, isn't it? Folks in high places can get you fired or get you hired. Just like that."

"It's not the same thing, Annie."

"Oh, I know that—and I don't mean to speak of Jessie in the same breath with those people. I—oh, Lord, Ki, I don't know what I'm saying anymore!" Her eyes blurred again, and

49

Ki moved quickly to her side. Annie buried her head in his shoulder. Ki slipped his arm around her and held her close.

"I—I gotta say something," she said quietly, "and it's real hard to say it."

"What, Annie?"

"About . . . you and me. The other night."

Ki groaned to himself. "Annie, you don't have to say anything at all."

"I do, though!" She turned her face up to his, brown eyes wide and pleading. "I just want you to know I had too much to drink. I don't . . . *give* myself to just any man that comes along."

Ki wasn't sure what to say. "Annie. You know we didn't actually, ah—"

"I'm not making excuses. I *wanted* to do it. With you, I mean. The drinks just loosened me up some." She sighed, and kissed him lightly on the cheek. "Oh, Ki, I can't tell you how it was. When you were . . . inside me and all, I came so many times I lost count!"

Ki was speechless. *My God,* he thought, *she doesn't know it all happened in her head!*

"Would you . . . like to do it to me again, Ki? Would you? Right now, I mean?" Her hands worked frantically at the neck of her blouse. Her breath came quickly, and there was a slight flush to her cheeks.

Ki sat up straight. "Annie . . . there's something I think you ought to know about the other night. Something I don't think you're really aware of."

"Oh, I'm very much aware of *everything* about that night," she purred in his ear. *"Everything,* Ki."

"Yes, but—"

"No, don't move. Just sit right still." Annie stood quickly and moved a step away, then finished loosening the buttons down to her waist. Slipping the blouse off her shoulders, she shrugged the chemise she wore under it over the tips of her breasts and down to her waist. The firm little mounds popped free with a jaunty bounce. As Ki watched, her nipples swelled to hard pink buttons. Annie gathered her skirts and slid onto his lap. Cupping the luscious breasts in her palms, she offered them up to his mouth.

50

"There," she whispered, "just for you, dear. Take them, Ki."

"Annie—"

"Lord, Ki, *kiss my nipples—please!*"

One dusky peak was only inches from his mouth. Ki gave up with a sigh, circled his arms about her, and brought her to him. His lips drew the soft and pliant flesh into his mouth. Annie screamed with pleasure. Her whole body trembled. She thrashed violently against him, gasped for breath, then collapsed with a sigh in his arms.

Ki stared in disbelief. She was sleeping gently, her lips curved in a pleasant little smile . . .

★

Chapter 7

Jessie finished lunch, thought about indulging in one of the Windsor's fine desserts, and decided against it. Leaving the dining room, she hurriedly crossed the broad marble lobby to the stairs. She saw the man coming out of the corner of her eye. Something warned her he was moving straight for her, and she turned instantly to face him.

"Miss Starbuck? Uh, is it all right if I speak with you for a moment?"

Jessie stared a full second before she knew who he was. "Why, Senator Hall? Sorry, I guess I wasn't expecting to see you again."

"No, I don't suppose you were." He looked straight at her, with flint-gray eyes flecked with blue. "That's one of the reasons I came. To apologize for my behavior."

Jessie studied him a long moment. He looked entirely different than he had the night before, and she heartily approved of the change. He wore denims, scuffed boots, and a frayed cotton shirt. In his hands he carried a Stetson the color of a dusty road.

"Your apology is accepted," she said evenly. "And what's

53

the other reason you came, Senator?"

"I want to talk," he said soberly. "If you will. I thought maybe we could get a couple of horses at the stable. If that's all right with you."

"That's fine with me." Jessie smiled. "I think a ride in the fresh air would do me a world of good."

Though the city was growing fast, Jessie noted that it still took only a few minutes to leave it behind. Marcus Hall spoke little until they were well out on the flats north of town, the blue-gray shadow of the Rockies looming on the horizon.

She'd traded her formal daytime gown for the clothes she liked best: a blouse of cream-colored silk, a pair of tight jeans, and cordovan boots. When she joined him back in the lobby, her brown Stetson hat framing a tumble of amber hair, Marcus Hall had taken her in from head to toe. There was no mistaking the bright gleam of approval in his eyes, and she'd caught the same look more than once on the way out of town.

"I hope you really meant that," he said finally. "About accepting my apology, Miss Starbuck."

"I did," she said, "and I like 'Jessie' better than 'Miss Starbuck.' Do your friends call you Marcus or Mark?"

Hall made a face. "In Washington, they call me a lot of things I wouldn't repeat to a lady. Marcus, though, will do just fine." He flicked the reins of his wide-chested gelding and slowed nearly to a stop. "I guess I'm kind of stubborn, Jessie, but I know when I'm wrong and I don't mind admitting it. I was wrong last night." The flint-gray eyes touched her briefly. "That story in the paper set me back. I was angry—mostly at you, I guess. When you tried to show me that picture..." Hall's voice seemed to break, "Damn it, I knew if I looked at the thing I'd see something I didn't want to see!"

"And *did* you look at it, Marcus?"

"Someone picked it up where you dropped it, and yes, I saw it. It was Marie, of course. A Marie I never knew, but it couldn't have been anyone else." He faced her, and looked deeply into her eyes. "I want you to tell me about her sometime. The way you knew her, as Lynnie. Who she was and what she was like. Not now, though. I don't think I'm ready for that."

"Yes. I understand."

Marcus looked at his hands. "You're not going to like this, but I have to be honest with you now. I believe the woman I loved was pretending to be someone else. Why, I don't know. But I do *not* believe the rest of it, Jessie. Marie was not murdered. Her heart simply stopped. She wasn't well at all. I think she'd been extremely ill for some time and couldn't bring herself to tell me."

Jessie turned in the saddle and stared. "Lord, Marcus—sick with what? Lynnie was the healthiest woman I ever knew!"

"I don't know." Marcus shook his head. "When I first met her in Cheyenne, she had a sinking spell or something. She was in the hospital for several days."

Jessie looked puzzled. "Cheyenne? I thought you met her here," she said carefully. "Didn't the Forsmans introduce you?"

"Oh, yes. She was Barbara's close friend. But Lane and his wife were in Cheyenne for a campaign dinner when I met Marie. Lane and I were both speakers."

"And she got sick there?"

"They think it was a slight heart attack. The disease was . . . beginning to take her."

Jessie could scarcely believe her ears. It was all she could do to keep from betraying her feelings, letting him see the astonishment in her eyes. "Can we stop awhile?" she said suddenly. "I think I could use a drink of water."

Marcus looked at her curiously, but quickly reined his mount under the shade of a sandstone outcrop. Jessie eased out of the saddle and Marcus joined her, handing her a canteen. She took a grateful swallow and handed the canteen back. For a moment she watched the sun on the distant peaks. She turned then and faced him again, hands locked solidly on her hips.

"You're wrong," she said flatly. "Even if you don't want to believe it, it's true. They murdered her, Marcus."

Angry patches of color touched his cheeks. "That's ridiculous. She never hurt a fly!"

"No. I don't think she did."

"Then it doesn't make sense, does it?"

"It happened. It doesn't have to make sense."

Marcus's eyes narrowed. "In the paper, you said the people who tried to kill you were responsible for Lynnie's death. Who, Jessie? Just who *are* these people?"

Jessie hesitated. Marcus saw the caution in her eyes and let out a breath. "Oh, well, fine," he said sourly. "This conversation's going nowhere at all, is it?"

"Will you tell me something, Marcus?" She turned, sweeping a tumble of copper hair out of her eyes. "Who told you about Lynnie's heart trouble? It obviously wasn't Lynnie."

Marcus shook his head. "No one told me. Not while she was alive. After she died, Dr. Sacchetti confirmed it."

"Doctor who?"

"Andrea Sacchetti. He's Lane Forsman's doctor. Hell, I guess he's everyone's doctor in Denver. Everyone who can afford him. He's Mrs. Culbertson's physician, too. You probably saw him at her place. Little sawed-off character. But a very fine doctor," he added hastily.

Jessie felt a chill touch her spine. "No, I— Who saw Lynnie in Cheyenne, when she was in the hospital there?"

"Why, Dr. Sacchetti."

"What was *he* doing there?"

"Traveling with the Forsmans. He's a family friend as well as a doctor, and he—" Marcus stopped abruptly. Understanding suddenly dawned in his features, and his eyes flashed with anger. "My God, you must be out of your mind. You're trying to bring Lane and Barbara into this, aren't you? Christ, they ought to put you away somewhere!"

"Now look, mister!" Jessie stuck out her chin. "If you loved Lynnie at all, you wouldn't run so fast from the truth!"

"Which truth is that?" Marcus snapped. "The real truth, or the one in your head?" Turning on his heel, he stalked to his horse and hoisted himself into the saddle. "Good day, Miss Starbuck. Sorry I took up your time!" Without a glance back, he spurred the mount savagely and bolted onto the flats.

Jessie watched him, anger coursing her veins like a storm.

"Great," she muttered darkly. "Thanks a hell of a lot for the ride!"

Jessie took her time riding back. Behind her, the mountains shone brightly in the afternoon sun. The outskirts of Denver lay just ahead—five or six miles at the most, unless they'd ridden much farther than she thought.

"Pigheaded bastard," she cursed to herself. "So damn certain

56

he knows all the answers!" She was relieved that she hadn't gone any farther. Lord God, in another few minutes she'd have told him what she knew about the cartel, showed him the small piece of cloth Lynnie had sent her. Jessie shuddered at the thought. She was certain he was on his way now to tell Forsman and his wife everything "that crazy Starbuck woman" had said.

She skirted a dry river and reined her mount to the east, remembering that the high bluffs ended farther on, allowing an easy crossing. An ancient river had cut through the flats, grinding a narrow channel some sixty feet deep. The sun painted curving ribbons of stone a deep ocher. Guiding her horse closer to the rim, she leaned out in the saddle and peered over. The canyon was too narrow to show her the bottom.

Jessie started as a bright thread of silver flashed under her eyes, grazing the horse's mane. Almost immediately, a second whisper of light followed the first. Her mount suddenly stumbled and went to its knees.

Jessie cried out, clawed empty air. The cliff streaked past her in a blur. Her hands scraped stone, found a solid spur, and held on. The action wrenched her hard, nearly tearing her arms from her shoulders. Jessie swallowed her pain and stretched her other hand quickly past her head to better the grip.

Desperately she worked raw fingers into the crevice, kicking blindly with her boots to find a hold. Her right foot touched a protruding stone. The stone snapped abruptly, leaving her hanging. Jessie took a deep breath and let it out slowly. Ki's familiar words rang in her ears:

Panic will kill you quickly. Sweep all thought from your mind and let reason take control . . .

She forced herself to trail her eyes down the cliff and look below. Her heart nearly stopped when she saw the horse. Its neck was broken, its body twisted at a terrible, awkward angle, forelegs held stiffly in the air.

Damn it, don't look at the horse! Look at your feet, Jessie, your feet!

Pushing back her fear as best she could, she searched the rock below for a foothold—anything to take the terrible weight off her hands. She could last another minute or two at the most . . .

She spotted a patch of shadow cast by a narrow lip of stone

57

beside her left knee. It was less than half an inch wide, but the rock looked brittle. If she could kick a little loose, just enough to take her toe...

Sweat stung her eyes. Her fingers trembled with pain; she could feel them giving way, the tortured tendons slipping. Jessie gave a desperate cry and kicked wildly at the face of the cliff. The stone wouldn't give; it was much too hard and she'd never work it free...

Suddenly her right hand gave way. Jessie screamed as her left took the full weight of her body. *Oh, God, I'm going ... I'm going right now!*

"Jessie—up here, quickly!"

She jerked her head up painfully, and saw Marcus's taut features twenty feet above. The looped rope tumbled down the face of the cliff, hit her shoulder, and fell away.

"Marcus, I can't!" she cried. "I can't ... hold ... on!"

Hall didn't answer. He drew the rope in hurriedly and dropped it again. This time the loop slid past her shoulders, toward her legs. Jessie grasped the rope to her, twisting her free arm about the cord, placing one foot in the loop. The stone beneath her left hand crumbled. Jessie fell two feet, then jerked to a halt. Hall began slowly hauling her up. Jessie closed her eyes and hung on.

When he eased her over the edge, she crawled weakly away from the rim and collapsed. Hall went to his knees and took her in his arms. Jessie looked up and smiled weakly. "Why— why did you come back? Not that I'm complaining..."

"I don't know," he said evenly. "I just did. Lord, Jessie, when I heard you yell, I thought— What the hell happened, anyway? Did a snake spook your horse?"

Jessie's green eyes flashed. "No, goddammit, not unless it had two legs. You can believe what you want, but they tried to kill me again!"

Marcus Hall looked at her without expression. "How, Jessie? There's no one around here, and no place to hide."

Jessie almost told him that she was certain now; she knew how they'd murdered poor Lynnie. "Forget it," she said aloud. "My horse had one of those heart attacks, Marcus!"

★

Chapter 8

Jessie bit her lip as Ki gently rubbed the salve into the torn flesh of her hand. When the balm worked into her skin, the sting went away and left a cool, soothing tingle, like the rush of spring water.

"Lord, that feels good," Jessie sighed, sinking back into the cushions of the couch. "You are a real wonder, old friend."

"Fine," Ki said stiffly. "Just try to remember how you got this way, Jessie. If you'd stayed right here—"

"—like you asked me to," Jessie finished. "I know, and I'm sorry. I thought maybe he knew something that would help." She sat up straight and looked at him. "And he does, Ki. He doesn't know it, but he does. That doctor. Andrea what's-his-name . . ."

"Andrea Sacchetti." Ki gave her a rueful look. "We are not going to discuss it again, Jessie. It is out of the question."

"All I want you to do is go to Cheyenne," Jessie sighed. "Just one day. That's all. You'll be back the next. They covered their tracks here, but I don't think they'll be expecting us to

59

check Cheyenne. Lynnie was in a hospital there, and I want to know why. There's got to be some kind of record. Brad Diamond can pull some strings for you, and Art McTavish. He knows everyone in town, and—"

"Jessie . . ." He drew up a chair and faced her. "There are a number of Starbuck interests right here in Denver. If you want to pull strings—"

"No. I don't trust anyone in this town right now. I'm sorry, but I don't."

Ki made a noise. "All the more reason for me to stay right here."

"Ki . . ."

He shook his head adamantly. "There is only one reason I would ever refuse you, Jessie. If my actions would put you in danger. Leaving you alone here would do just that."

"Are you going to follow me around all day and night?" she said glumly. "For the rest of my life?"

"If I have to, yes."

"Huh! You could at least *talk* about it."

"There's nothing to talk about. I'm not going, Jessie, and that's that."

Ki walked down the swaying coach, making his way along the aisle to the next car. It was close to eleven o'clock; the dim glow of a single lamp yellowed the sleeping passengers' faces. There were six cars in the train—all coaches and no Pullmans, though one of the cars was fitted with private compartments. The lack of a sleeper made his job a little easier, but the compartments presented a problem. Only three besides his own were occupied. One held four cattlemen who seemed determined to play cards all night. He had no idea who was in the other two.

Moving through the last car before his own, he let his eyes touch each of the sleeping figures. There was a drummer in a checked suit and a derby, a farm couple and their young child. There were several cowhands and a man who looked like a merchant. Near the end of the car, an old Indian woman sat alone, a blanket pulled over her nodding head. Like all the other passengers aboard, the ones in this car looked perfectly harmless.

Opening the door to pass between cars, he paused a moment to peer out into the night, then entered his own coach. After making sure the door to his compartment hadn't been disturbed, he opened it and locked it behind him, then sprawled out on the horsehair seat. A moment later he stood briefly to douse the light. No use making himself a target unless he had to.

Ki knew, of course, that all his precautions were useless against a really determined foe. If assassins had followed him aboard, they'd look like innocent strangers—drummers, farmers, maybe the loud cattlemen two doors down. And if they cared to break down his door— He shook his head as he regarded the thin wooden panel.

He slumped down despondently in his seat and folded his arms, a scowl creasing the taut flesh of his brow. "You were a fool to let her talk you into this business," he muttered darkly. "You should be back in Denver where you belong!"

If she hadn't agreed to let him talk to Marshal Vail, he would never have given in. Now, at least, two of the chief marshal's deputies would stick to her like glue while he was gone. Vail had been happy to help. Ki knew he felt badly because there was little else to do, and he'd jumped at the chance to lend a hand.

But it's not the same, and you know it. You should be there. You should be there, right beside her!

Annie's heart nearly stopped when he paused beside her seat. He wasn't two feet away; she could feel his eyes right on her! After a moment he moved on, opened the door to the next car, and disappeared. She sighed and pulled the blanket a little closer about her head. In the morning she'd sit real quiet until he got off the train and it pulled out again. *My God,* she thought with a chill, *what if he doesn't get off at Cheyenne? What'll I do then?*

The tears welled up and scalded her eyes. She remembered waking up and finding him gone, and knew it had happened again. It was always the same, ever since she'd known little girls were different from boys. Just *thinking* about a lover inside her was almost enough to trigger her off. If he kissed her, touched her anywhere at all, the honey-warm furnace between her legs simply exploded and sent her reeling. When she came to again, the man was gone. Sometimes she tried to tell herself it didn't happen that way at all. In her heart, though, she knew very well it was true . . .

Ki was the last straw. She liked him more than a little, and knew she couldn't face him again. Losing her job made the decision real easy. Packing a small satchel, she'd walked out of the room and straight to the depot, bought a ticket on the first train out, and sat down to wait.

Ten minutes later, Ki walked in. Annie nearly passed out on the spot. The Indian woman was sleeping two benches down, the blanket folded neatly beside her. Annie snatched it up, left half a dollar in its place, and draped the heavy cover over her shoulders . . .

She woke with a start and glanced wearily out the window. The flat plains to the east were smudged with gray; the sun would be up in an hour, and soon after that they'd be in Cheyenne. Closing her eyes, she shifted her weary frame and dozed again. Almost at once, she jerked awake with a start. There was a sound—a sound that didn't belong. She turned to peer back along the car. Nothing. The other passengers were sleeping. Startled, Annie looked up and realized the noise was coming from directly over her head.

"Lord God," she muttered under her breath, "someone's up there. Someone's *walking* on top of the car!"

Slipping out of her seat, she moved along the aisle to the vestibule door. There was no light at all, only the pale glow of dawn against the sky. Through the glass in the door, she could see the small space that separated her car from the next. *Ki's back there,* she thought to herself. *In one of those compartments.* She wondered if he was awake, if he—

Annie pressed herself flat against the wall, her flesh suddenly as cold as ice. A shadow had appeared through the glass— and then another and another. She watched in horror as they slipped silently off the roof and onto the platform between the cars. There were three of them, dressed in coal black from head to toe. They paused for only a moment, like a part of the darkness itself, then vanished swiftly into the car beyond.

For a moment Annie stood rigid, unable to move. Then the truth suddenly struck her like a blow.

Ki! Oh, Lord God, it's Ki they're after!

Without thinking at all, she threw open the door, ran to the door to the next coach, jerked it open, and screamed out Ki's name. The man in black loomed up before her, hit her in the face, and sent her sprawling. Annie gasped, and tried to claw her way to her feet. The man picked her up and slung her roughly over his shoulder. Annie cried out. Suddenly the outside door was wide open and the night was rushing by. One of the men jumped and disappeared, and then the other. The man who held her grabbed her arms, lowered his shoulder, and tossed her away.

Annie screamed. She was falling through the night, with nothing beneath her. She hit hard, tumbled head over heels, and lay still. A ball of flame exploded behind her, turning the night blood red. Annie gasped and opened her eyes. A small part of a second before she sank back into darkness, she saw the car vanish under a blinding curtain of light...

Just before dawn, Jessie tossed the tangled sheets aside and crawled wearily out of bed. Thoughts of Lynnie's death had plagued her mind half the night, mixing with fears of her own. Once, she'd come awake with a start, her body bathed in a film of cold sweat. In a dream, she'd fallen off the cliff once again—only this time the wall was as smooth as glass, and she'd screamed all the way to the bottom...

"I sure as hell don't need this," she told herself shortly. "I can get more rest standing up!"

Slipping into her clothes, she brushed her coppery hair in the half-light, then moved across the bedroom to tap lightly on the door to the parlor. The door opened instantly and the young deputy marshal looked past her, his hand touching the Colt at his hip.

"Everything's all right," she told him. "I just couldn't sleep. I'm afraid it was one of those nights."

"Yes'm," he said politely. "Thought I heard you tossin' around. You, uh, want me to send down for breakfast?"

She read the touch of caution in his eyes, and knew the suggestion had come from Billy Vail. "No," she said firmly, "I am *not* having breakfast up here. Go round up your friend. We're going to hunt up the best steak and hotcakes we can find—outside this hotel. My treat, too."

The deputy suppressed a grin. "Whatever you like, Miss Starbuck."

It was nearly eight when the two men trailed Jessie out of the Columbine Cafe and into the already busy street. The clerk at the Windsor had given her directions to the city library; she had no trouble tracking it down, or finding the books she needed. There were several good volumes on medieval weapons, books with pictures of enormous battering rams, catapults, and ballistae. There were halberds, pikes, and wicked-looking axes of all kinds; one of the latter looked remarkably like the hatchets her attacker had used.

Jessie's heart skipped a beat when she came to a section on crossbows. She'd seen one of the weapons before, in a museum. It looked very much like something between a rifle and a bow. The bow was made of steel, set crosswise in a wooden stock. The bow was bent by a crank windlass, placing the steel under tremendous pressure. The weapon fired a short steel bolt with such power that it had become the most dreaded weapon of war for a hundred years.

I was right, she thought soberly. *Only it wasn't a steel bolt I saw out there. It was something long and needle-sharp!*

She remembered the first bright flash, then the second whisper of light that had squarely struck its target. If she was right about the weapon, its missile had driven straight to the animal's brain, killing it in an instant. It was there in the horse's skull at the bottom of the canyon—not that anyone would ever care to look.

Jessie read on, turning to a section on more subtle weapons of the Middle Ages. There were poison rings that dropped a tiny pinch of powder in the cup of a prince, rare and deadly herbs that killed quickly without a trace—or left a victim in agony for days.

When she found what she wanted, she nearly cried out. There it was, a stark and ugly picture of the thing that had killed her friend. *Oh, Lord, Lynnie! I wish I could have been here—I wish I could have done something to help!*

Closing the book with a sigh, she stood and crossed the room to the door. The two deputy marshals rose and joined her. *Damn,* thought Jessie, *if I'd ever even mentioned to Ki what I was thinking, he'd never have gone to Cheyenne—he wouldn't have let me out of his sight...*

They were on the street when she saw Marshal Billy Vail making straight for her. The look in his eyes stopped her cold. She knew in an instant what he would tell her. She wanted to turn and run, to do anything but face him.

"Let's get back inside," he said soberly. "I have to talk to you, Jessie."

"No!" Jessie tore out of his grasp. "It's Ki, isn't it? I *know* it's Ki!"

Vail gripped her arm, guided her into the library, and sat her down in a chair. "I'm sorry," he said grimly. "He's gone, Jessie. Ki's dead."

Jessie squeezed her eyes shut and gripped the chair. "You're wrong. He—he's not... I know he's not!"

"Jessie." His big hand covered her own. "I'd like to be wrong, but I'm not. It happened right above Greeley. On the train. Someone blew the car he was in clean away. Some others were killed too. We don't even know how many. The explosion was a bad one."

Jessie shook her head. "He might not have been there. You don't know Ki. If you haven't actually found him—"

Vail cut her short. "Jessie, listen. They haven't found much of the whole *car,* damn it! I'm sorry. He's gone."

Oh, God, Ki! The tears finally came. Billy Vail held her, trembling, against his shoulder. Not for the first time, he wondered why he hadn't done what his pa had told him, and bought a nice saloon or a store...

When she came out of the bedroom, her cheeks were flushed and her eyes were swollen, but she was calm—almost eerily calm.

"There's something else I've got to ask," said Vail, "if you feel like talking. If you don't, it can wait."

"Something about Ki?"

"Maybe. I don't know." The marshal leaned forward in his chair. "About the time I got word of all this, a friend on the Denver police came by. He knew you and Ki were friends of this reporter from the paper—Annie McCullough."

"Annie?" Jessie sat up straight. "What about Annie, what's wrong?"

Vail looked at his hands. "I expect you know she lost her job."

"Yes, yes, Ki told me."

"She left her room late last night. Her landlady found the door standing open and called the police. It doesn't look like she took much with her. She just walked out and didn't come back."

"Oh, Lord!"

"You don't think she'd have got on that train with Ki, do you?"

"No." Jessie shook her head firmly. "Ki went to Cheyenne on business for me. He wouldn't have risked Annie."

"Yeah, well. Someone that could've been her bought a ticket, but of course that don't mean it was." Vail looked at her a long moment. "Jessie, you mind telling me what it was you sent him up there to do?"

Jessie hesitated, then told him about Lynnie's stay in the hospital in Cheyenne, and about Dr. Sacchetti's connection with the Forsmans.

Vail growled and made a face. "Damn it, Jessie, are you still on that? Why don't you just—" He caught himself, and the color rose to his face. "Sorry, I got no right to talk to you like that. Especially not right now."

Jessie reached out to touch his hand. "It's all right, Billy. It doesn't matter much anyway, does it? Ki's dead, and there's nothing that'll bring him back to me now."

Less than an hour after Billy Vail left, Jessie marched out of the Windsor to the stable down the street. Her two guardians protested, but Jessie wouldn't listen. If they didn't ride with her, they could let her alone—and neither one cared to face Billy Vail and tell him that.

It was just past noon when she arrived at Elaina Culbertson's ranch. A Mexican maid ushered her in, and Jessie strolled boldly into the parlor, a deputy U.S. marshal on either side. Elaina Culbertson looked up, startled. For a moment her features went slack, then she quickly forced a smile.

"Miss Starbuck, what a pleasant surprise! You should have let us know you were coming."

"Just out for a ride, and I thought I'd drop by," said Jessie. "Hope you don't mind? Oh, Mrs. Culbertson, these are Deputy U.S. Marshals Cooper and Delaney. Marshal Vail won't let me run loose without them, after what's been happening, you know."

"Uh, yes—of course." Elaina smiled weakly from her chair. "Please sit down, gentlemen. And your . . . other friend, Miss Starbuck? The Oriental gentleman? Oh, dear, the name escapes me now."

"Ki," Jessie said flatly. "His name was Ki, and he's dead, Mrs. Culbertson. Someone blew him up on a train just this morning."

Elaina Culbertson's eyes went wide. "Lord, child, what are you *saying!*"

"Miss Starbuck—is this true?"

Jessie turned to see Senator Lane Forsman at the entrance to the room, his wife just behind him. Barbara stared, then hurried to a table and poured the shaken Elaina a glass of water. Lane stalked up to Jessie, his face as dark as a stormcloud.

"What happened?" he demanded. "Tell me."

"Someone killed him," said Jessie. "Threw a bomb or something in his compartment. Ki's dead—and everyone else who was anywhere near him."

"Damn!" Forsman laid a hand lightly on her shoulder. "If there's anything at all I can do . . ."

"I'm sure Miss Starbuck will tell you if there is," Barbara said coolly. She thrust herself between her husband and Jessie, and gave Lane a killing look. Forsman went red, started to speak, and decided against it.

"I think you and I need to talk, Miss Starbuck," Barbara said. "Just the two of us."

"Fine," said Jessie. "That might be a good idea."

Barbara Forsman turned and left the parlor, leading Jessie down a narrow, stuccoed hall. Through an open window, Jessie glimpsed an old stone fountain, and realized it was the patio where Elaina Culbertson had held her party. Barbara stopped at a small anteroom that held nothing but a heavy Spanish chair and a narrow bench. She nodded for Jessie to sit, and turned to face her.

"Will you answer something truthfully?" she said abruptly. "You didn't just happen to ride by here, did you? You came deliberately."

"Yes," Jessie admitted. "You're absolutely right." She held Barbara's penetrating gaze. In spite of how she felt about this woman, she was enthralled once more by her breathtaking beauty.

"I knew that, of course. And I don't have to ask why. Marcus has told me how you feel. You think Lane and I—you think we're responsible for what happened to Marie." Her features went rigid and her eyes turned to fire. "I can't tell you how that angers me, Miss Starbuck. I find your accusations intolerable!"

"Well, I don't blame you for that."

"My God, how could you?" Barbara shook her head in dismay. "And poor Dr. Sacchetti. You're dragging *his* name through the dirt as well!"

"I asked Marcus who attended Lynnie during her illness. He told me." Jessie looked the other woman straight in the eye. "Mrs. Forsman, I don't believe for a minute that my friend died of a heart attack."

Barbara's face flushed. "I assure you, that is *exactly* how she died."

Jessie started to stand. "You know what? I don't think this conversation is—"

"Please! Just sit down and *listen*, damn you!" Her eyes bored into Jessie like daggers.

"I've told this to no one but Dr. Sacchetti. Not even Lane. Marie D'Avenant and Lynnette Harley *were* the same person. I didn't need the picture you gave Marcus to tell me that. *She* told me. Here, in Denver. And she told me why she pretended to die in London, and why she fled to France and changed her name." Barbara paused, and her full lips trembled. "Lynnette fell in love with an Englishman, a hateful man who used her for his—his sexual pleasure. For himself—and for his friends, when it pleased him. He kept her under his sway through drugs. In time, she became a hopeless addict to morphine, and I don't know what else."

68

"Oh, come now!" Jessie sat up straight. "I can't believe that of Lynnette."

"Believe what you like," Barbara said stiffly. "I assure you it's true. The fire in that London hotel was her doing. She set it deliberately, under the influence of drugs, to rid herself of the monster who'd enslaved her. A friend of her lover's, a man who was apparently less a devil than he seemed, spirited her away to France. She spent more than a year there, in an asylum. Under the finest care, she made a partial recovery and assumed a new name. It was after this that I met her."

"And she was no longer an addict?"

"No. Not then. I didn't learn her story until a few weeks before she died. She *had* to tell me, because I walked in and caught her administering the drug. There was little she could do but confess she'd succumbed to her addiction again."

"And this was in Cheyenne."

"Why, yes, it was." Barbara seemed surprised. "I hospitalized her there, under Dr. Sacchetti's care. You see, she *did* have a bad heart. Dr. Sacchetti thinks it was brought on by her long addiction. *That* is what finally killed her, Miss Starbuck."

"And Marcus knew nothing of this?"

"My God, no!" Barbara looked alarmed. "He met her and fell in love with her. I know I should have said something, but I simply couldn't!"

Jessie said nothing. Barbara Forsman looked up and met her eyes. "You don't believe any of this, do you?"

"I believe someone has been trying to kill me," Jessie said evenly. "I believe the best friend I ever had was blown to bits this morning and I'll never see him again. I'm trying real hard to see how Lynnie's heart attack made all this happen."

Barbara came to her feet, and her whole body trembled. "I don't know!" she cried suddenly. "I don't know anything anymore!"

Before Jessie could move, Barbara turned and fled, leaving her alone in the small room. Jessie stared after her. She wasn't sure what to think. The woman certainly *sounded* convincing— as if she really believed what she was saying.

Starting down the narrow hall, Jessie passed the broad window and the sunlit patio beyond. Suddenly, movement caught her eye. Turning quickly, she saw the girl at exactly the instant the girl spotted her. She was visible for only a second, but Jessie knew she wasn't mistaken in what she'd seen. The girl was very young and lovely, her flesh painted gold by the sun. Dark hair tumbled down her back like silk—and she was as naked as the day she was born.

Jessie stared, shook her head, and walked on. Suddenly a door to her left jerked open, and Lane Forsman marched toward her across the courtyard. His face was livid and his fists shook in anger.

"Damn you!" he shouted. "Just hold it right there! I don't know what you've done to scare Barbara, but I sure as hell intend to—"

His words were cut off by the unmistakable *splat!* of a bullet striking flesh, and almost simultaneously, Jessie heard the distant report of a rifle. Lane Forsman gasped and crumpled forward, a painful grimace having replaced the anger that had been on his face a moment before.

Jessie wheeled about in time to see a puff of smoke rise from the shadow of a boulder in the hills beyond the house. Deputy Cooper raced from the house, drawing his pistol as he ran. He dropped to one knee in the middle of the courtyard and emptied his Colt in the direction of the sniper, who was continuing to fire. Here and there, rifle rounds sang off the flagstone in little spurts of dust. Jessie dove to the ground, and felt rock fragments sting her cheek as a slug ricocheted off the fountain next to her.

Deputy Delaney sprinted frantically toward her, then his head snapped back and he was flung backward to the ground by a round that had hit him squarely in the forehead.

Abruptly, there was no sound at all. Then Barbara Forsman began to scream. Jessie looked up. The woman was kneeling beside the senator, staring at her hand, bright red now with her husband's blood . . .

Chapter 9

Ki slept . . .

He dreamed of a narrow valley between two emerald hills. The hills rose from the valley like the swell of a woman's breasts. The trees and the sky sparkled. It seemed as if the very air itself were throbbing with color . . .

He paused at a diamond-blue spring and bent to drink. A breeze wafted down from the hills . . .

Ki suddenly froze. Cool liquid spilled from the cup of his hands. The wind brought him the hot and fetid breath, the smell of rotten meat . . .

Tiger! He could feel the great beast's presence, sense its fiery eyes. It was close, moving swiftly toward him on pads of velvet . . .

He woke with a start, his body covered with sweat. The sky was the color of ash, the landscape dark and indistinct. He sprang to his feet, bent over in a crouch, and tried to quiet the frantic rhythm of his heart. The dream was gone, but the tiger was still there; he could see it, feel it, smell its awful presence.

It had happened to him before—the dream pulling him up out of sleep to let him know that danger was near. It was *kime*, the sixth sense that had no name. It brushed the edge of his mind, showed him the ghost of his enemy's face. *The thing was close now, close enough to kill!*

Ki moved—even before he heard the woman scream, before he heard their feet whisper toward his door...

He leaped to the window, slammed it up hard. The door behind him shattered. Out of the corner of his eye he saw shadow against shadow, a face without features. Something bounced off the horsehair seat and rolled to the floor...

He threw himself out the window as the world exploded behind him. White heat seared his flesh. The dawn brightened to noon. Somewhere in the corner of his mind, he wondered idly why he couldn't hear his own ragged cry...

He opened his eyes and looked at the sun. It was six, he guessed, maybe a little after. The first thing that struck him was the silence. He choked and tasted blood, raised a hand and wiped his mouth and saw that the blood was from his nose. Reaching past the plane of his cheek, he touched his ear. There was blood there too. The explosion had deafened him, then. He'd seen it happen to men before, and knew it usually went away.

He raised himself slowly on his arm. The pain hit him hard and slammed him back. *I think I've broken my back!* he thought dismally. Gritting his teeth, he tried again. Trembling on one supporting arm, he stared down at his legs. The left was all right. The right was twisted at an awkward angle. He moved it gingerly, felt the pain race up his leg. Likely not broken, he decided, but he'd have a hell of a time walking for a while.

Taking a deep breath, he blinked and shook the cobwebs out of his head. He was sitting in a thick clump of sage at the bottom of a gully. At the top of the gully was the railroad embankment, and the tracks. Ki looked again, and his belly shriveled in a knot. The blast had thrown him a good thirty yards, slammed him against the bank, and rolled him into the brush.

When he saw the train, he wondered why the hell he wasn't dead. Debris was spread a good hundred yards along the track.

72

The engine and the first two cars were unharmed. So were the cars at the rear end. The third was nothing more than iron wheels and charred butts of timber.

Horses and wagons were pulled up beside the tracks; men scurried about, searching through the burnt wreckage.

The strips of his shirt that he'd wound tightly about his ankle helped him walk, but the pain was still there. Easing himself from cover, he edged casually into the clearing and mixed with the others. No one seemed to notice. He walked quietly to the rear of the crowd, to the wagons and waiting horses. Easing himself gently on a big gelding, he let it take him down the gully and out of sight.

Jessie would think he was dead.

He hated to do that to her, but there was nothing else for it. He'd found their tracks and knew they were heading due west. Finding the right sign had taken a good two hours of circling about, but he was certain he was right. They'd gotten on the train when it slowed for a grade, probably walked along the tops of the cars. One man had followed with the horses. He found where they'd mounted up again, run east for half a mile, then crossed the tracks once more, heading west.

There were three horses, one of them likely riding double. Ki wondered about that. If there were four men, there should have been four horses. Maybe one had gone lame farther back.

He wished he knew exactly where he was. Past Greeley, he decided, close to the Wyoming border. The next two hours took him through broad, open grassland, flat prairie country with few trees at all. The men were moving fast, but Ki made no effort to match their pace. He had a good idea where they were going. The high peaks of the Continental Divide shimmered just above the horizon—twenty-five, thirty miles to the southwest. He stopped a moment and studied the land ahead. His first guess had been close to right. The explosion had taken place where he'd figured. Any farther north, and the Divide would be much more to the west.

Just before the flats gave way to the foothills of the Rockies, he came to a narrow, steep-walled canyon. Nearly a thousand feet below, white water tumbled away to the east. Reaching the water helped. Though he'd never seen it before, he knew he'd found the Big Thompson River.

73

As the land began to rise, juniper and sage gave way to steep, wooded slopes stretching up to far peaks. Soon he was climbing north of the river through thick forests of Ponderosa pine and Douglas fir. The pain in his ankle was less intense—he could handle that, force it out of his mind. The loss of his hearing was something else. That made him vulnerable to the men who'd tried to kill him.

An hour into the hills, he spotted a thin column of smoke through the trees, and worked his mount slowly up the ridge. A gaunt, narrow-eyed man stepped out to meet him, a Greener shotgun cradled in his arms. Behind him, Ki saw a small cabin, with a woman and three spindly youngsters peering at him from the window.

Ki knew he wasn't welcome inside, and didn't ask. Still, the mountaineer was willing enough to trade Ki's winded horse for an animal half as sound. Before he left, Ki gave the man a dollar, and got a sack of bread and dried venison in return.

He led his mount up the steep, spiny ridges, keeping well north of the river. The Big Thompson was a different river here. It was still strong and lusty, but no longer left deep rocky gorges in its wake.

When the sun disappeared behind the high peaks to the west, shadow came swiftly to the land. Before night set in, Ki found a site for his camp. From the sign on the trail, he knew the others weren't far ahead. The terrain had slowed them down, and they'd be stopping early, too.

With sundown, the cold came quickly. He'd lost his rope-soled slippers in the explosion, but he didn't need them. He'd used his shirt to bind his ankle, and there was nothing he could do about that. His worn denims and leather vest were little comfort, but his camp was out of the wind, and the horse's saddle blanket helped some.

Well before dawn, he was up and in the saddle, chewing a strip of meat and crust of bread. His hearing was much better, almost back to normal. As soon as he could see the ground clearly, he pushed the mount hard, circling northwest away from the river, then doubling back south. He'd kept a cold camp, but he doubted that the others had done the same. As

74

careless as they were about their backtrail, they likely wouldn't worry about a fire.

While he rode, Ki took a quick inventory of his possessions. The job took no time at all; the small satchel he'd taken on the train was still back there—probably burned to a crisp. He'd carried several razor-edged *shuriken* throwing stars in the pocket of his vest, but had lost them in the fall, along with the slender, curved knife he usually carried in the waist of his trousers. His *surushin*, a five-foot length of slender rope, was still intact, its lead-weighted ends wrapped twice about his waist. It was a useful weapon, but he wasn't certain at all that he could use it. His back still hurt, and his ankle would severely limit his mobility. Normally he was confident with only his hands and his feet for weapons. Now he knew they might fail him. There were three men up ahead, and maybe a fourth. One, he knew, was the man he'd sensed in the alley, the intruder who'd nearly taken Jessie's life. He was a man Ki was most anxious to meet, but not without the full use of his body. When it was time to settle their quarrel, he'd have to bring all he could muster to the fight. If he didn't, the other would kill him with the speed of a snake.

Rounding a pink outcrop of granite, he brought his mount to a halt. The smell brought a slight smile to his features. Coffee, and the salty tang of bacon. He led the horse back down the trail for a good fifty yards, then started back up the slope, his bare feet touching only solid stone. The effort cost him dearly, but there was no time to worry about it now.

Working himself up the ridge, he eased himself over a flat shelf of rock. A stunted spruce had spidered its roots across the stone, and he was grateful for the heavy curtain of foliage. He could hear them; they were thirty, maybe forty yards away. A pan rattled over the soft rush of the river. One man spoke to another. It was a language Ki didn't know—Russian, maybe, or some Slavic tongue.

Carefully he spread a cluster of spruce needles aside. One man squatted by the fire. Ki spotted the arm of another behind a rock. A third stood looking over the river. When he turned, Ki's body went rigid. The sun seemed to fade and leave him cold. *This is the one*, he thought with absolute certainty.

75

The man at the fire spoke again, and the man by the river walked toward him. From a distance, Ki got the impression of broad, heavy features and hooded eyes. His hair was cropped short, and his ears seemed overly small for his round, bulletlike head. Like the man at the fire, he was dressed in black trousers and a loose black shirt.

The few steps to the fire told Ki a great deal. He remembered his dream of the tiger, and knew it hadn't hit far from the truth. Standing still, the man looked blocky, a little above average height, a man with too much fat on his bones. When he moved, Ki knew this wasn't so. He was a man who'd thrown a hatchet from each hand after Jessie's bullet struck him, and come all too close to the mark. He was a man in command of his body. It would do what he asked, and do it well. Walk, climb, kill without effort. Everything he did was a natural act, a—

Ki suddenly stiffened, and his eyes went wide, as the man he'd seen behind a rock suddenly moved. Only it wasn't a man at all, it was Annie McCullough! How in hell did she—

Ki's mind raced. The missing pieces suddenly fell into place. The woman's scream, the four riders and only three horses. *There's another man here, then. Where the hell is he?*

Ki didn't stop to think, or wonder what Annie had been doing on the train in the first place. The third man was wandering around somewhere, and Ki had to find him.

Sliding along the rock the way he'd come, he eased himself back to solid ground, setting his good foot ahead of the other. To his left was a thick stand of spruce. The river was to his right. Ki paused, listened, and moved quickly to his left. There was a wooded ridge down below; if the man had left camp, he'd likely pass that spot, coming or going from whatever errand he was about. Ki walked deftly from one stone surface to the next, making sure he left no tracks behind. Nearing the ridge, he pulled himself carefully around a boulder—

The man looked up, startled, facing Ki less than four feet away. His hand moved quickly from the buttons of his pants, snaked the Colt from his belt, and aimed it straight at Ki's head.

Ki moved in a blur.

His right leg was bent slightly at the knee, while his left swept out in a killing arc. The man cried out as the edge of

76

Ki's foot broke his wrist. The Colt clattered away; Ki spun in a full circle and thrust his left hand up like a blade. His palm caught the point of his foe's chin and snapped it back. The man went limp. Ki caught him before he fell, searched about and found the Colt, picked it up, and jammed it back in the man's belt.

Ignoring the hot lance of pain that tore at his ankle, he lifted the man in his arms, crossed quickly below the outcrop to the bank of the river, and tossed his burden to the rocky shore below. The drop was a good twenty feet. A rattle of small stones followed the body. Ki paused, then loosened a section of bank and sent it tumbling. His legs were weak, and sweat stood out on his brow. A tall spruce hung over the river, and he grasped it to keep from falling. There was no time left, and he knew it. The others had heard their friend cry out. In another few seconds they'd be on him. He'd never make the safety of the trees—he'd fall before he even got close.

His eyes searched desperately about the clearing—the river, the high upthrust of stone. Glancing overhead, he squinted along the straight trunk of the spruce. A stubby branch shot out a good six feet over his head. Above that, the foliage was thick and dark. In a single motion he loosed the slender coil of the *surushin* from his waist, held one end, and whipped the other in a circle. The *surushin* whirled once, twice—Ki jerked his arm up fast. The weighted end of the rope caught the branch and spun tight. With a quick glance over his shoulder, Ki pulled himself up by his hands, grasped the branch, and swung his leg over it. Belly down on the branch, he loosed the *surushin* and snaked up the tree as far as he could go.

He heard the others almost at once. They spoke in low tones, the harsh, foreign sound of their words reaching up to his perch. One called out softly and brought the other running. They'd found the body sprawled in the stream. The picture Ki had painted was easy to follow. The man had stood too close to the edge. A section of loose rock had given way, and he'd fallen and broken his neck. There, see? That's where his boot hit the bank . . .

Ki waited and listened. The man who'd sat by the fire stayed above; the big man climbed down to look at the body. In a moment he joined his friend and they both moved away. Ki caught a quick glimpse of them through heavy foliage, walking back to their camp.

Ki held his breath and didn't move. He could read the other's thoughts as well as his own, and knew the man had circled back without a sound, knew he was standing below the tree right now, listening and waiting. Ki could feel him, almost see the corded muscles of his back, hear his soft and steady breathing. He was reading the ground, trying to capture the scene in his mind, make it happen again. Had the man really fallen—or was there something else to see? A print that shouldn't be there at all, a twig snapped on the path . . .

Ki waited, silently thanking the caution that had made him leave his mount far below in the trees. If he'd brought it any closer . . .

It was a good half hour before the man moved again. Finally, Ki heard him stepping over rocks and through the brush, moving off toward his camp. Ki grinned. The man was making a hell of a lot of noise—which meant he wasn't leaving at all. In a moment he heard the rattle of pots in the camp, gear being stowed in the packs. Finally he heard the horses move off upriver.

Ki's foot throbbed with pain; his whole body ached from holding the cramped position. Still, he didn't dare move an inch. He waited an hour, two hours. His mind was now one with the other's. He imagined he could hear the beat of his heart, feel the surge of blood through his veins. He knew exactly when the man moved quietly away. He made no sound; Ki simply knew he was gone. Rubbing feeling back in his limbs, he climbed painfully down the tree and dropped to the ground. Glancing at the sun, he guessed the man had stood below without moving for a good three hours . . .

Late in the afternoon, the high stands of fir and spruce began to thin, as Ki climbed close to the granite peaks of the Divide. The sky was a brilliant blue, the air thin and sharp in his nostrils. An hour before, he'd seen an abundance of elk and deer. Now there was no game in sight, and no good cover to keep them safe.

And none for me, either, Ki thought to himself. Soon he'd have to venture into the open, follow the trail up the barren fields of stone. If the men guessed he was there, it would be a simple thing to kill him. All they had to do was wait; sit back and let him walk under their sights . . .

Ki swept the thought aside. There was another thing that bothered him more. The men had Annie. Considering the shape he was in, Ki wasn't at all sure he could free her, even if he managed to get in close. One, maybe. But the other wouldn't be that easy. It would be like killing a hawk in its sleep.

And if he did get her—then what? Ki was certain the pair were headed for some hidden retreat in the mountains. If he kept on their trail, they'd lead him right to their masters, the men who'd killed Lynnette Harley and now wanted desperately to put Jessie out of the way. If he tried to get Annie, take the two before he learned where they were going—

Ki cursed aloud and slammed his fist against the saddlehorn. He couldn't risk her life. He would wait, but not too long. If the right moment came, he'd have to take it . . .

Evening darkened the eastern slope of the Divide as he reined his mount to a halt on a steep granite spur. A few lone spruce and alpine fir clung to the harsh gray landscape below. Above, high over the peaks, a golden eagle etched an impossibly blue sky. Ki wondered how the hell he'd get through the night without freezing, and knew he didn't dare try. He had to cross the Divide before dark. Gritting his teeth against the chill, he tried to picture a map of the Colorado Rockies. Now the Big Thompson was only a cold mountain spring at his back. He guessed he was ten, maybe eleven thousand feet above the shadowed plains to the east. There was a pass, somewhere nearby. Miller? No, *Milner* Pass, that was it! If he was right, it should be in sight now, north and a little to the west. Was that where the others were headed? He decided it had to be, and urged his mount forward.

Ten minutes later he saw them.

They were across a rocky valley, nearly five hundred feet above his path. Ki counted the dark figures, and breathed a sigh of relief. Two men, and a smaller figure that had to be Annie. Now she had a horse to herself, tied to the saddle of the mount ahead.

They were all there. No one was waiting, bellied down

behind a rock with a Winchester. Ki waited until they vanished below the ridge, then spurred his horse forward. They had to be headed straight for the pass. He was glad they knew the way, since *he* sure as hell didn't.

When he reached the spot where the men had disappeared, Ki's mount stumbled and nearly fell. A small shower of stones rattled down the face of the mountain, and Ki frantically jerked the horse back to the right. The animal trembled; Ki dismounted and tried to quiet it. He'd been afraid of something like this from the beginning. The horse was old and used up. He was surprised it had taken him this far. Now the high country and its rarified air were taking their toll. He could keep on riding and risk a fall that might kill him—or try to *walk* down the westward spine of the Rockies. It was a hell of a choice, next to no choice at all. His ankle was somewhat better, but certainly not ready for a hike. He'd have to ride the poor creature until it dropped, and hope for the best. If he didn't, he'd lose the others for sure, and maybe cost Annie her life in the bargain.

Leaving the horse, he walked a few steps along the ridge, then went to his knees and crouched at the edge. For a moment his heart nearly stopped. The horses were gone—vanished in thin air! Frantically, Ki searched the barren granite peaks. His eyes found a deep cleft less than half a mile away. It had to be the pass—Milner, or another he didn't know. He let his gaze follow the western slope of the Divide. He could see bare granite for miles, and no sign of riders.

Suddenly he let out his breath. There they were—a high ridge had hidden them from view. Ki squinted at the white ball of the sun. There was another hour of light, maybe even two. They'd make it down before dark, but he'd have to wait, give them a good start. If he rushed it, they'd look back and spot him for sure. Which meant the night would catch him on the treacherous heights of the mountain, on a horse nearly ready to give up the ghost . . .

Ki woke, burrowed out from under his deep cover of branches, and stretched stiff limbs. Peering through the trees, he saw the faint glimmer of dawn behind the high granite wall. He forced himself to stand, gingerly testing his ankle. The sleep had done

80

him some good; he was sore, but the swelling of his ankle had gone down a great deal. Taking off the strips of bandage, he rubbed the tender muscles a long time, then bound the ankle tightly again. Walking wasn't bad, but Ki had no illusions about his strength. The wrong kind of strain, and he'd fold in an instant.

He ignored the ache in his belly, and settled for a swallow of water. He'd wolfed down the last of the bread and venison the night before, and didn't regret it. After his harrowing trip down the mountain, he'd needed food badly. The horse had amazed him, getting them down without breaking both their necks in the dark. Half frozen from the chill mountain air, he'd stopped at the first stand of trees, stripped every full branch he could find, and crawled under the pile. It was no feather bed at the Windsor, but it was better than freezing to death . . .

The horse gave him a long, baleful look, and groaned as he climbed in the saddle.

"If I could buy you a whole sack of oats, I'd do it," Ki said solemnly. "You've earned it and then some, friend."

The day was bright and clear, the morning sky filled with billowy white clouds tinged with pink. Ki kept to the edge of the woods, peering at the lush mountain meadows. The foothills below were covered with flowers—columbine, harebell, and aster in a hundred shades of blue. He took it slow and easy, knowing they'd likely camped close by. Even with a good head start the evening before, they wouldn't have gone far.

He spotted them just after eight, riding south on one of the tree-covered foothills trailing to the west. As he watched, the riders turned abruptly east, heading back toward the mountains. Ki's mind raced. There was no reason to do that at all—unless they were close to where they were going. And if they were . . .

He kicked his mount forward, plunging down the hillside into the valley as fast as he dared. If he knew where they were going, he could ride ahead and meet them, perhaps get Annie free before they reached their destination.

If he got her out alive, he'd have to kill them both first— he knew that for certain. After what the pair had done, that suited him fine. He'd take their lives without blinking.

He kept the horse at a slow, easy lope along the floor of the valley. After a good two miles, he climbed back up through the trees to the crest of the hill. If he was right, the men who had Annie would come riding along just beneath him. Easing off his mount to the ground, he made his way through the brush, loosening the *surushin* from his waist. He'd take the stocky man first, then—

Suddenly, Ki stopped short, and whirled about in his tracks. A branch snapped behind him and below. He frowned, puzzled at a noise where a noise shouldn't be. Turning, he hurried back the way he'd come, the weighted rope dangling from his hand. Passing the thicket where he'd hidden his horse, he climbed a tumble of rocks and looked southward. For a moment the sight stunned him. His eyes could see it clearly, but his mind struggled to bring it into focus. Splitting the hill beyond was an immense wall of stone, a ragged spine of granite that had thrust itself nearly two hundred feet above the earth. Perched atop this crest was a sprawling stone fortress, a structure that looked to Ki like the ancient Indian ruins at Mesa Verde or Canyon de Chelly. This dwelling, however, had not been built of adobe—it was made from the same ashen granite that formed the small mountain below.

Pulling his gaze quickly from the sight, Ki searched the hillside beneath him, knowing instantly what had happened. He'd expected the riders to move west; instead, they'd turned off southward for the island of stone while he was racing to cut them off. Movement caught his eye. There—below and to the right, coming out of the trees. A smile creased his features. He could still catch them, get Annie before they came in sight of the rocky retreat.

Running back to his horse, he hurled himself into the saddle and urged the mount roughly down the hill. There was no time for waiting in ambush now, hoping to catch the pair off guard. He'd have to hit them hard, and hope for a second or two of surprise.

His path led down into deep, twisting gullies covered with Ponderosa pine. He was thankful for the terrain; it would let him get closer, mask the sound of his approach, right to the end. The trees thinned and the land went flat. Suddenly he saw them, ahead and just below. As his horse crashed through the trees, he looped the weighted *surushin* in his fist. The stocky man looked up, startled by Ki's sudden appearance. The rope

82

whirred, and sped in a crazy arc for the man in black. He ducked to one side, tried to throw himself off his mount. He was fast, but the *surushin* was faster. The weighted rope tightened in a blur about his thick neck and shoulders. The man cursed as he tumbled from his horse. Ki ignored him, heading for the startled Annie McCullough. The second man quickly danced his horse in front of Annie, and levered a shell into his rifle's chamber. Ki kicked his mount straight at the gunman, drew his right hand back, and chopped the man hard across the chest. Ribs snapped under the blow. The man cried out and slipped to the ground.

Behind Ki, Annie McCullough screamed. Too late, Ki kicked his mount aside. Strong hands circled his waist, pulled him out of the saddle, and slammed him to the ground. Ki took a blow on his shoulder and rolled free, coming to his feet in a fighting stance. The stocky man looked at him and grinned, tossing the tangled *surushin* to the dirt. Ki saw his face closely for the first time—pale, almost colorless blue eyes, features as hard as gristle. Without taking his eyes off Ki, he reached for his belt and came up with a hatchet in his fist.

Ki backed off. The man stalked him, soft boots scarcely making a sound. He tucked his head low on his shoulders, waving the weapon lightly in his hands.

"Go, Annie," Ki said tightly. "Get out of here, *now!*"

Annie shook her head, ground her teeth, and kicked her horse straight for the man with the hatchet. He sensed her behind him, danced aside, and swung the ugly weapon in a blur. Annie shrieked; her mount went to its knees, a fountain of blood pulsing from the slash in its neck. Annie tumbled from the saddle and Ki moved fast. The man turned to face him, bringing the hatchet about in a wicked circle. Ki sucked in his belly, felt the razored edge kiss his flesh, then lashed out hard with his feet. The man took the blow on his belly, grunted, and stumbled back.

Ki wasn't fooled. The blow hadn't hurt, and the stumble was no more than a feint. Ki countered with a feint of his own, thrusting a fist out quickly and drawing back. The man fell to a crouch and came in low and fast.

Ki spun fully about, smashing his foot solidly into the other's ribs. His foe went down, and this time Ki knew the pain was

83

real. The big man rolled frantically to get away. Ki moved in relentlessly, hurting him again and again, kicking every soft spot he could find. The man covered his head, took the blows, and rolled to his feet.

Ki backed off and glanced at Annie McCullough. She was gasping for breath behind the horse. The animal shuddered and bled its life away. The man with the hatchet came at him. Ki let him come. The other was fast, incredibly fast and agile for his size, but Ki kept half a breath ahead. He waited now for the weapon to swing again, for the man to put his strength behind the blow. He watched the colorless eyes, the thick cords in his throat.

The man moved—but Ki moved a split second sooner, ducked under the vicious arc, and chopped up hard with his left. It struck the man's throat in a killing blow, but his uncanny senses warned him in time. He pulled back, shook his head, and came in again. Ki hit him hard across the chest. The man's face constricted in pain. Ki danced aside, formed a wedge with the knuckles of his fist, and went for the bridge of the nose. One blow would finish it; the man would die before he ever hit the ground . . .

Ki slammed his foot against the earth and came in fast. Pain shot like a hot metal lance up his leg. The ankle gave way. Ki stumbled, caught himself, then tumbled to the ground. The other read his weakness in a second, and turned the odds around. A boot slammed viciously into his ribs, another into his belly.

Ki rolled, fighting desperately to get to his feet. The man stood above him, his broad features creased in a grin. "Now!" he said in harsh, broken English. "Now I hurt you plenty goddamn bad!"

★

Chapter 10

It was well after sundown when the deputy U.S. marshal in the hall knocked lightly on Jessie's door to tell her Marcus Hall wanted to see her. Jessie's first thought was to send him away. The last thing she needed was another useless argument that would undoubtedly get right back to the Forsmans. Still, the man was somehow part of the puzzle, and personal feelings were something she couldn't afford at the moment. Lynnie and Ki were dead. If Hall knew anything at all. . . .

"We need to talk," he said soberly. "I hope you don't mind, Jessie. I wouldn't bother you if I didn't think it was important."

Jessie was shocked by his appearance. His features were drawn, and he looked as if he'd aged ten years. "Come on in," she sighed. "Get yourself a brandy. You look like you could use it."

Marcus accepted her offer, poured himself a generous serving, and downed it in a swallow. "I'm sorry about your friend," he said without facing her. "What happened this morning. That's terrible. I didn't know him, but—"

"Marcus—" Jessie stood directly behind him, forcing him to turn and meet her eyes. "It has been one hell of a day, I don't mind saying. I've lost the best friend I ever had. This morning I saw another man die before my eyes. Both of them are dead because of me. I don't feel real good about that, and I don't much feel like talking."

Marcus looked away. "I can well understand what you're saying."

"Good. Now what is it you want to say?"

"There are some things I think we ought to get straight— things that have gotten confused between us."

Jessie looked pained. "There's no confusion at all, Senator. I tell you things in confidence, you turn around and spill them to someone else. *That's* what's the matter between us."

"I didn't mean any harm by that, Jessie."

"Fine. That makes it all right."

"Jessie, please—"

"Look, damn it—" Jessie caught her breath, then let it out in a sigh. "Oh, hell, all right. Yeah, we got off to a real bad start and you aren't responsible for all of it. I'm willing to try again, if you are."

She gave him a weary smile, and Marcus looked relieved. "Jessie, there's nothing I'd like better. Truly." After filling his glass again, he sank down in a chair. "I just got back from Elaina's place. They've been combing the hills all day for the sniper who killed that deputy and wounded Lane."

"And?"

"Nothing. No luck at all. Barbara's taking Lane out of here. They were having some folks out to their place next week, and Barbara's moved it up. She figured Lane would be safer up there." Marcus paused and looked at his glass. "I know how you'll take this, but she's asked you to come, Jessie. She's frightened now, scared out of her wits. I think she understands your situation a little better, now that this business has hit her personally. She doesn't understand how she and Lane are involved, but it's pretty clear they are. She'd like to try to talk to you again."

"I don't think I'm especially interested in talking to Barbara Forsman," Jessie said coolly.

Marcus didn't try to argue. "The U.S. marshal was out there most of the afternoon."

"Billy Vail. He was up earlier. I had to face him, and I don't think I handled it real well."

Marcus shook his head. "My God, Jessie, you can't blame yourself for what's happened."

"No? Then who do you figure I ought to blame, Marcus?" She walked over to him, pulled out a chair, and sat down, facing him squarely. "Look, that's one of the things that set you and me off right from the start. I told you what I thought about Lynnie. You didn't believe me. I'm sure you still don't."

Marcus looked at her. "Barbara told me what she said to you. About Marie's—Lynnie's— drug addiction. I knew nothing about that. Lord, it doesn't seem possible, but—"

"But you believe it, right?"

"Jessie, it makes more sense than a lovely girl like that getting murdered!"

Jessie moaned, stood, and threw up her arms. "My God, here we go again. Marcus, I know you'd like to think that what happened to me and what happened to Lynnie aren't connected, but it just isn't so. I guess I'm going to have to prove that to you before we go any further." Before Marcus could speak, she crossed the room and slipped a piece of paper out of the dresser drawer and brought it to him.

"I'm trusting you by sharing this, Marcus. To be honest, I didn't much want to before. Now I don't think I've got any choice."

Marcus looked bewildered. He picked up the paper and glanced at it quickly. His face went ashen and he stared up at Jessie. "Christ, what the hell is this?"

"It's what brought me running to Denver. You don't deny it's Lynnie's writing?"

"No, but . . . it doesn't make sense. Who's this Aunt Emma?"

Jessie blew a lock of amber hair out her eyes. "You better get yourself another brandy, friend. I think you're going to need it."

She told him the whole story, leaving nothing out. Hall had made a name for himself by rooting out corruption; more than once he'd heard vague rumors about a Prussian cartel, and he had little trouble accepting that part of her story. Jessie told him how her father had fought the faceless men most of his life. Marcus knew he'd been murdered, but was unaware of the reason, or of who was behind the killing.

"Ki and I have come up against these people before," said Jessie. "It's getting to where I can spot their hand in the game. That fellow with the hatchets, now. *He* fits in, for certain. And that 'accident' when you and I were out riding . . ."

Marcus started to protest, but Jessie went on, explaining the crossbow weapon she thought the man had used. "If you don't believe that," she said tightly, "you're not going to care for the rest of it. I think I know how they killed Lynnie. It's not very pretty, but if I'm laying all the cards on the table, you've got to have this part too. That bright silver flash I saw just before my horse went down gave me the answer. It's an old trick from back in the Middle Ages. I found several references to it in the library. You take a long needle—some thing like a lady's hatpin or a thin stiletto, and jab it through a person's ear, directly into the brain. Do it just right, and there's no way to tell how they died."

"Good God, Jessie!" Marcus shook his head in horror. "Do you know what you're saying? Who the hell would do a thing like that?"

"A doctor, maybe," Jessie said calmly. "Someone who knew human anatomy real well. Wouldn't be real hard for a man like that . . ."

"Oh, well, of course!" Marcus slapped a hand against his face. "We're back to the Forsmans again, and Sacchetti. I guess you've forgotten that Lane got shot today, too?"

Jessie didn't answer. She drew the embroidered snip of handkerchief from her pocket and dropped it in his lap. "I was saving this for last," she said darkly. "That symbol's the cartel's mark. There's no mistaking where it's from. It came with the letter, Marcus. Lynnie sent it to me."

Marcus looked at the thing for a long moment. When he brought his eyes up to meet hers, they showed no expression at all. "Who else knows about this?"

"Ki and Billy Vail. And Annie McCullough." Marcus looked blank, and Jessie explained, "She's a reporter for the *Rocky Mountain News,* a friend of Ki's and mine."

"Jesus." Marcus looked at his hands. "If—if all this is true, and anybody knows what you've told her, her life isn't worth two cents."

"I wouldn't worry about that," Jessie said sadly. "I think Annie McCullough's dead already."

It was close to eight when Marcus brought out his watch and realized they'd been talking for a good two hours. He offered to take Jessie to dinner, but they both decided it would be wiser to stay off the streets. The Windsor had a fine dining room, and could send up anything they wanted. Jessie and Marcus realized they were starved, and ordered everything from roast quail and mountain trout to New York ice cream and a platter of fruits and cheeses. When the feast was over, Jessie groaned and sank back in her chair.

"Lord, Marcus, maybe we should have gone out. I think I could use a good stroll. About twice around Denver." She looked at him and frowned. "Hey, we agreed to put problems away for dinner, remember?"

"I remember," Marcus said distantly, "but dinner's over, isn't it? You fed me a lot more than I can swallow, Jessie, and I'm not talking about food. *Why*, damn it?" He stood abruptly, his gray eyes darting angrily about the room. "What does this cartel want? What are they after?"

"You've asked the right question," she said wearily. "I wish I could give you an answer." A thought suddenly struck her, and she gave him a questioning look. "Marcus—does Elaina Culbertson have anyone else living out on that ranch with her? A granddaughter, a niece? A very pretty young girl?"

"No, I don't think so. Why?"

"You're not going to believe this, but just a second or so before the shooting started, I saw a beautiful girl across the patio. A very naked young lady."

"What?" Marcus said, puzzled. "Are you certain?"

"I know what a naked girl looks like."

"Must've been one of the servants." Marcus caught the look in Jessie's eye. "Lord, you don't think Elaina Culbertson's involved in this?"

"No, I don't. But the Forsmans are, I'm convinced of that. I don't care if Lane *did* get shot. I think Elaina Culbertson knows that too, Marcus. I've seen the look on her face once

89

or twice. She's scared out of her wits about something."

"That doesn't make sense," Marcus growled. "And we're getting off the subject, aren't we? Whoever's behind all this, what are they after? If Lynnie *was* murdered—God, they've killed four people. What for?"

"You can't believe Lynnie could get involved with such a thing, do you?"

"People who want to take over the country? No, I can't."

"I couldn't believe it of her, either," Jessie said gently. "I think maybe we're wrong, Marcus. I think she *had* to be involved. She wasn't the same person I knew years ago. And I think—I think her meeting you was no accident at all."

"Oh, come on, now—"

"No, listen. I think she made a mistake that cost her her life. I think she fell in love with you, Marcus. Maybe that was why she had to die."

Marcus didn't answer for a while. "Why, though?" he said aloud. "What would killing her accomplish?"

She knew the answer was there, somewhere, preying at the edge of her mind. But nothing would come, nothing to put a name to the cartel's madness. All she could think of was Ki, that she'd never see him again, that he'd never be there to talk to. Never...

Oh, God, she cried out inside herself, *I miss you so, Ki. I miss you so much!*

"You're trembling," said Marcus. "Are you all right, Jessie?" He moved closer to her and slipped his arm protectively about her shoulders.

Jessie didn't protest. She was suddenly cold and tired, and it felt good to have him near. "I'm all right, I guess. Lord, I'm scared, Marcus. I'm just plain scared, and I don't like that at all!"

"They're not going to beat us," Marcus said tightly. "Damn it, we won't let them, Jessie!"

"No!" She shook her head in desperation. "You don't understand, you don't *know* them! It's already happening, Marcus. It's happening now. They—"

"Jessie, stop it!" He suddenly drew her to him, pulling her roughly against his chest. Jessie gave a ragged cry and came into his arms. All the sorrow and the pain buried within her seemed to burst through at once. Her tears wet his lips as he covered her face with kisses. His touch brushed the corners of her eyes, trailed down her cheek, and found the softness of her mouth. Jessie sighed and opened her lips to his caresses. She felt her pulse quicken under his touch. The fiery kisses flowed through the length of her body, tingled in her breast, and warmed the secret places between her thighs.

Marcus sensed a hunger within her that matched his own. He rose from the sofa and lifted her in his arms; Jessie's hands snaked eagerly around his neck as he carried her swiftly from the parlor to the bedroom beyond.

She looked at him, a soft and lazy smile on her lips. Not a sound passed between them. It was as if they both knew this was not a time for words. Marcus sat on the bed beside her. His hand touched her cheek, brushed the ivory column of her throat, and trailed to the swelling cleft of her breasts. Her nipples grew hard under his gaze. Jessie groaned and thrust her breasts up to meet him, the taut little buds stretching the fabric of her blouse. His fingers found the row of pearl buttons and loosed them quickly. When his hands reached her waist, he reached up to slip the blouse off her shoulders. Jessie smiled and sat up, covered his eager hands with her own, and slid her legs over the side of the bed. Loosening two hooks at her waist, she gathered her skirts and brought them rustling past her legs, up to her thighs.

"Now," she said softly, "I'll leave the rest for you, Marcus."

Marcus needed no further invitation.

Jessie stood while he slid the silken fabric down her thighs. With a whisper, it brushed the length of her legs down to her ankles. Jessie stepped from the frothy circle, a mischievous gleam in her eyes. Marcus Hall's breath caught in his throat. He'd undressed Jessica Starbuck a dozen times in his mind; still, the sight of her there before him sent a bolt of raw hunger to his groin. She wore nothing but a creamy white chemise, a garment that ended just at mid-thigh and clung to every curve and hollow.

The ivory-handled derringer, in its garter of red satin, was a surprise. Jessie caught his look and grinned. "A girl can't be too careful," she told him.

"If you think *that's* going to keep me away . . ."

"Senator Hall, I'm not even going to try."

She stood with her legs pressed together, hands locked demurely below her navel. The posture gave her a shy-little-girl look—it also bowed her shoulders and let the narrow straps of the garment slide down her arms. The pale fabric hung precariously on the points of her breasts, boldly baring the rosy tops of her nipples. If she moved now, risked even half a breath . . .

Jessie could feel his gaze upon her; his eyes branded her flesh as they took in every inch of her body. She took a step toward him and closed her eyes, bringing her hands to her sides. The filmy slip fell away, exposing the full, upturned curve of her breasts.

"Tear it away," she told him, the words hissing between her teeth. "Please, Marcus!"

His hand brushed the hollow between her breasts, grasped the cloth, and ripped it free of her body. Jessie sucked in a breath and opened her eyes. He came to her, and crushed her firmly to his chest. The rough fabric of his clothing was strangely exciting next to her skin. She could feel the strength of his erection against her belly. She rubbed herself playfully against him, molding the hollow of her pelvis to his shaft.

Marcus gave a quick cry of pleasure. Before she could guess what he was doing, he clutched the slim circle of her waist and lifted her easily off the floor. Startled, Jessie saw the flash of his smile, laughed aloud, and scissored her legs around his waist. Running long fingers through the copper coils of her hair, she arched her back against the pressure of his hands. He bent to touch the taut globes of her breasts, to take the swollen tips between his lips. Jessie cried out with joy. She cupped her breasts gently in her hands, offering them up for kisses. His mouth encircled the rosy peaks of flesh, drew them eagerly into his mouth. His touch ran like fire through her body, smoldered in her belly, and raced down the length of her legs. His tongue teased her nipples, flipping the pert buds until each small touch made her shudder.

"Marcus, I can't stand any more!" she cried aloud. "Take me now—please!"

Marcus's flint-gray eyes looked amused. "That'd be kind

of hard to do, Jessie, seeing as how you're all naked and I'm not."

"Well, if that's what's holding you back," she said sharply, "we can sure fix it fast!" Loosing her legs from his waist, she sprang to the carpet and started tearing at the buttons of his shirt. While she worked, Marcus explored the plush curve of her bottom, and let his hands slide around to her belly and down to the soft nest below.

"My God," gasped Jessie, backing off quickly from his touch. "If you start that, we're going to be here all night!"

"All night'll be just fine with me."

"It's fine with me too, but that's not what I meant. Marcus, I . . . oh, Lord, what are you *doing!*"

Marcus laughed and lifted her in his arms. Once more he carried her to the bed, gave her a hefty swing, and dropped her. Jessie shrieked, bounced on the feather mattress, and came to her knees.

Marcus looked at her and stared. "Damn, Jessie—don't move," he said dryly. "Just stay right there. Just like that . . ."

"Like what?" Jessie asked coyly. "You mean like this?" Arching her back like a cat, she thrust her bottom in the air and gave it a twitch. "I guess that's what you mean. Can't imagine why you'd want me to do that . . ."

"Just hang on a minute," groaned Marcus. "I'll explain the whole thing."

Jessie gave him a saucy laugh. "Somehow I think I've already got a fair idea."

Marcus stumbled out of his trousers, tossed them across the room, and came to her. Jessie watched him over her shoulder, through a veil of amber hair, saw the hard lines of his body, the dark, matted hair of his chest. His shaft stood boldly erect, and she trembled with pleasure at the sight.

"Lord, you are a *beautiful* man!" she sighed. "Oh, Marcus, I *need* you so, do you know that? Do you?"

Marcus didn't answer. He moved up behind her until his thighs touched the luscious swell of her hips. Jessie moaned and dug her knees into the bed. He stayed where he was, the hilt of his erection resting just at the edge of her treasure, the swollen tip brushing her navel. Then, grasping her hips, he leaned away slowly, letting the hard shaft trail past her belly to the sweet, honeyed warmth between her thighs. Jessie cried out as if he'd pressed a hot brand against her. "Oh, yes, yes!" She bit her lip and shuddered at his touch. Once more, Marcus brought his member close, brushed the feathery moistness, and pulled away.

"Marcus!" Jessie thrust herself at him, trying desperately to draw him inside her. Marcus held her back, his hands pressed firmly against her bottom.

"I hope you're enjoying youself," she said darkly. "I'm about to go crazy, and you know it!"

"Uh-huh. I know." He grinned at the curve of her back, the lovely swell of her hips. "I know, Jessie, because you're driving me out of my mind. Lord, you are a beautiful woman. I've never in my—"

"Well, if you haven't," she snapped, "don't you think it's about time you did? Marcus, I want you inside me, and I want you there now!"

"You do?" Marcus tried not to grin. "Well, why didn't you say something?"

He slid past the warm, silken flesh and sank deep inside her. Jessie trembled beneath him, her hands clawing desperately at the sheets. Sucking in a breath, she matched his thrusting rhythm with her own. He drew her to him with his hands, pressed her back, then drew her to him again. Her body filled with his warmth, bringing her ever closer to the delicious flood that would take her and carry her away. She could feel it coming closer, like the roll of faraway thunder. She knew, too, that he would join her when the storm gathered her in. She could feel him growing inside her, swelling her satiny walls with every thrust. She could almost read his thoughts, and knew he was making no effort at all to make their loving last. He knew their need was too great, their hunger too intense for that now.

Jessie let herself go, gave herself to the heat that was rising up within her. His pelvis slammed hard against her bottom, as he drove himself frantically inside her.

Suddenly Marcus bellowed and clutched her to him. Jessie gasped with delight. His orgasm filled her loins with fire. It surged through her body like one great explosion after another, loosening her own hot pleasures and sending her soaring. A

94

long and ragged cry escaped her throat as she rose to dizzy heights of sweet release. A mixture of pain and joy twisted her features, drained the strength from her limbs, and left her trembling. When the last, almost unbearable wave of ecstasy swept through her thighs, Jessie shuddered and went tumbling along in its fury. Her legs gave way and she collapsed on her belly, too weak to move anymore. Marcus's erection slipped from her grasp, but the heat of his pleasure smoldered within her. He took her in his arms, turned her over gently, and drew her to him. Their bodies were slick with a thin film of moisture. He kissed her, and the rich, heady scent of their love reached her nostrils.

"That was lovely," she whispered, "very lovely, Marcus. We must have needed each other a lot."

"Oh, yes. I think we did, Jessie," He looked at her, snuggled close against him, the delicious length of her body honey-gold in the half-light. "I think we needed to let ourselves know we were alive. Making love is something that says that very well. We were . . . oh, God, Jessie, I'm sorry!"

"Marcus . . ."

He closed his eyes and tried to turn away. Jessie stopped him, and brought him around to face her. "Hey, there's nothing wrong with remembering people you loved." She smiled through her own tears, bringing a finger to his lips. "It's all right to think about Lynnie and make love to me. Don't you know that?"

"Yeah, I guess it is. Anyway, I can't really help it. It's there."

"Of course you can't. Any more than I can stop thinking about Ki. We didn't have this kind of love, but we had something very special, Marcus. I feel the same kind of emptiness about Ki that I do about Lynnie. They're gone, and that means a part of me's gone too. Oh, God, hold me again, will you— *please* hold me!"

He brought her against him, kissing away her tears, and when their lips met again, Jessie drank him in with a fierce and desperate hunger. Marcus soothed her, warming every tender hollow with his touch. He kissed the warmth of her throat, let his lips trail over the firm flesh of her breasts. Once more he feasted on the musky taste of her nipples, stroked them with his tongue, and made the dimpled flesh grow hard.

He lingered there a moment, then brushed his mouth along her velvet skin to the swell of her belly. A thin line of down led from just below her navel to the silken mound below. His mouth brushed lightly over the moist, feathery curls.

When he kissed the creamy hollows of her thighs, Jessie stirred and gave a lazy little sigh. Gently, Marcus parted the curly nest with his fingers, exposing the delicate folds hiding below. Jessie shuddered at his touch; she spread her legs wide to welcome him in, the tips of her toes trembling against the bed. The motion opened her up like a flower, baring the heart of her passion. Marcus marveled at the beauty before his eyes. The lovely sight quickened his pulse, hardened his rigid member even further. He bent to kiss her then, letting his lips brush the satiny, coral flesh. His tongue slid gently over the shell-pink pearl at the crown of her treasure. Jessie writhed uncontrollably, and the firm little nub swelled at his touch. The tangy wine of her loins assailed his senses, heightened his desire, and sent a fresh surge of blood through his veins.

"Oh, yes, yes, *yes!*" Jessie cried. "Kiss me there, Marcus, kiss me!" Her hands came down to grip his hair, pressing him roughly to her thighs. He plunged his tongue deep inside her. Jessie's body arched in a bow; she jerked wildly against him, her breath coming in rapid little bursts. Marcus found every secret hollow, every luscious corner of her pleasure. Jessie gasped for air; her mouth went slack and a vein throbbed rapidly in her throat. Her face was slick with moisture, her skin a blush of scarlet.

Marcus could wait no longer.

The white ball of fire within his loins threatened to swell and take him under. He brought himself to his knees, slid up the length of her legs, and thrust his erection inside her. Jessie cried out with joy and came up to meet him. The first touch of his member triggered the storm churning within her. Her body went rigid, then exploded with sweet release. Her face was a mask of pain and pleasure. Marcus gasped as the walls of her loins spasmed frantically against his erection. His head snapped back as the orgasm caught him up and carried him away. He groaned with delight as the flood within him surged deep inside her, again and again and again . . .

"What time do you think it is?" whispered Jessie. "Two, maybe close to three?"

"Later than that," yawned Marcus. He stretched and peeked at the windows beyond the bed. "Why, do you have another lover coming at three?"

Jessie groaned and made a face. "Lord, Marcus, if I do, I don't know what I'm going to do with him!"

"I know what *I'm* going to do with him," Marcus said grimly.

Jessie laughed and nuzzled his ear. "Want me all to yourself, do you?"

"Yes. I don't much feel like sharing."

"Neither do I. Feels too good just like it is . . ."

Marcus kissed her tenderly. Jessie grinned, made a little noise, and closed her eyes.

"There's something I want to say," he told her. "Maybe you don't care to hear it, but I've got to say it anyway, Jessie."

"Hmm, what's that?"

"An awful lot's been happening the last few days—to both of us. Maybe I shouldn't tell you this at all, but it's something I want you to know. Jessie, I loved Lynnie a great deal, and I don't think I'll ever forget her. What we've had between us, though, you and I—it's something Lynnie and I never shared. I wanted to, and I think she did too, but we— Jessie?" He leaned close to her, and in the pale light he saw she was sleeping soundly. With a sigh, he took her in his arms and nestled her head against his shoulder.

Jessie woke with a start, cold fear welling up inside her. "Marcus," she cried, reaching out to find him. "God, Marcus, there's someone here. I can hear them, in the parlor!"

Marcus was already on his feet, heading for the door.

"Don't!" she warned him. "Wait, Marcus!" The ivory-handled derringer was in her fist, and she was reaching out to stop him as the door burst open.

"Police," the man snapped. "Drop that, lady, or I'll shoot!"

Jessie froze as they suddenly filled the room, their pistols leveled at her head. She tossed the weapon aside and clutched the sheet to her breasts.

"Goddamn it!" Marcus exploded. "What the hell do you think you're doing!" He fumbled about for his trousers, jerked them up to his waist, and advanced on the nearest policeman.

"Stop right there, mister." The officer drew back the hammer of his Colt, and Marcus stopped.

"All right, hold it." A heavyset man in a black suit and derby hat pushed the officer's pistol aside. "You two get on back in there. I'll handle it." The pair left, and the man in the derby stepped up to Marcus. "My name's McHenry. Sorry, folks, we got us a little problem, I reckon. You Senator Marcus Hall?"

"Yes, I'm Senator Hall," Marcus snapped, "and you've got more goddamn trouble than you can handle. What in the—"

"Just a minute," McHenry said calmly. He glanced at Jessie and cleared his throat, making an effort to keep his eyes off the tantalizing bit of thigh at the edge of the sheet. "Are you Miss Jessica Starbuck?"

"Yes, I am," said Jessica. She glanced warily at Marcus. Marcus came to her and touched her arm.

"Get dressed, Miss Starbuck," the lawman said flatly. "Now, please."

Jessie flushed. "I will not! Not until you get yourself out of my bedroom!"

"Sorry. Can't do that. Use the screen, ma'am."

Marcus started to protest, but Jessie shook her head. Pulling the sheet about her, she stalked behind the screen and quickly slipped a dressing gown over her shoulders. When she was finished, the man in the derby nodded toward the door to the parlor. "Out there, please. Both of you."

Jessie gave Marcus a puzzled look, stepped into the room, then shrank back at once, gasping. The parlor was a shambles. Chairs were turned over, the carpet bunched up in a ragged mound. The room was littered with empty bottles. Jessie smelled stale champagne and the sweet odor of bourbon.

"I don't know what's been going on out here, but I demand an explanation!" blurted Marcus.

The man in the derby looked at him with cold blue eyes. "Fine, Senator. We're lookin' for the same thing, then, aren't we? Would you two step over here?"

Jessie and Marcus exchanged bewildered looks. They walked

around the back of the sofa as the officer directed.

"Oh, Christ!" Marcus's face twisted in horror. He turned quickly to hide the sight from Jessie. Jessie shook him off and squeezed past him. Bile rose to her throat, and the room swam dizzily about her. She clutched the edge of the sofa and sucked in air.

The girl was young and beautiful. She lay naked on the floor, sightless eyes staring at the ceiling through a tangle of wheat-colored hair.

"She—she's dead, isn't she?" Jessie stammered.

McHenry gave her a look. "Yeah, she's dead," he said flatly. "Must've been one hell of a party, huh?"

"Goddamn you!" Marcus's face was purple with rage.

"Christ." The man looked from Marcus to Jessie, as if he had a bad taste in his mouth. "You rich bastards make me sick to my stomach!"

★

Chapter 11

It was well past noon before Jessie and Marcus left the squat
brick building that housed the Denver police headquarters and
the city jail. Billy Vail led the way, hustling them out the back
door to a waiting carriage, his bearlike form and booming voice
threatening anyone who stood in his path. The alley was only
a little less crowded than the street out front. Jessie figured
half of Denver had shown up to get a peek at the "scandalous
couple."

Marcus Hall muttered under his breath as Vail's deputies
on horseback cleared a way through the crowd. When the
carriage was finally free and clattering south, Jessie reached
out and laid a calming hand on his arm.

"It's all right," she told him. "It's over. We won't have to
go through *that* anymore."

"No?" Marcus's face was flushed with anger. "Hell, it's
only just starting. Damn!" He ground one hand into the other.
"How could those fools even imagine we'd be capable of something like that? It's—it's incredible!"

Jessie sighed and sat back. "Marcus, that's not the point, and you know it. It doesn't matter whether the charges stick or not. I'm sure the cartel never expected it to go any further than it did."

Marcus gave a harsh little laugh. "They sure know their politics, Jessie. They'll crucify me in California and Washington. After this, I couldn't get elected cattle inspector."

Jessie's green eyes flashed. "Marcus Hall, you're a good man and a fine senator. They won't forget what you've done or who you are."

Marcus shook his head. "You're wrong, I'm afraid. Last night's what they're going to remember." He turned to her, and his gray eyes softened. "Hell, I have no business worrying about myself. You were there too, and I'm afraid your reputation is—"

"My reputation is my business," Jessie said firmly, "*I* know who and what I am, and that's all that counts. I meant to make love to you, Marcus. And I figure that goes for you too. The rest of that business didn't happen."

"Tell *them* that," Marcus said wearily, nodding vaguely over his shoulder.

She knew, of course, that he was right. A juicy scandal was much more interesting than the facts, and the story might well end Marcus's career. She could imagine the next day's headlines in the *Rocky Mountain News:* BEAUTIFUL GIRL DIES IN SENATOR'S LOVE NEST TRIANGLE! NIGHT OF SIN ENDS IN DEATH; STARBUCK HEIRESS INVOLVED!

The story would spread all across the country, and the cartel would get exactly what they wanted. Unless Marcus could mend fences quickly, the voters would laugh their "corruption fighting" senator out of office—on the grounds that he knew entirely too much about his subject.

Though the day was hot and sultry, Jessie felt a sudden chill. Sometime in the night, the minions of the cartel had murdered a young girl in cold blood, quietly arranged a death scene, then tipped off the police. *Lord*, she thought darkly, *they killed her because they needed a body, with no more thought than swatting a fly . . .*

* * *

102

Billy Vail paced the small room. The house was comfortable and clean, far on the outskirts of town, on the poorer side of Cherry Creek. Jessie was grateful for his help. The idea of returning to her suite at the Windsor was almost more than she could bear.

"All right, let me lay a couple of things out," said Vail. "They don't know who the girl is, or where she's from. My guess is that she was working at one of the houses on Holladay, or in the back room of a saloon." He looked at Jessie and cleared his throat. "I still got some friends on the Denver police—did have, anyway. So I know how she died. Alcohol poisoning, pure and simple. Someone forced a bottle of whiskey down her throat. That's not all, either," he added grimly. "She was, uh... sexually molested. Used pretty bad."

"Oh, God!" moaned Jessie.

Marcus cursed under his breath. "So what happens now, Marshal?"

"Not a damn thing," Vail said flatly. "Hell, Josh McHenry knows you folks didn't do anything to that girl. He's bull-headed, but he's not stupid, and of course he couldn't just ignore the fact she was up there in your room and dead. If he figured you two were guilty, I'd never have been able to drag you loose."

"You went out on a limb, and we're grateful," Marcus said firmly. "I know local lawmen get itchy about federals messing around in their business."

"They do for a fact," beamed Vail. He gave Marcus a sheepish grin. "Thing is, I know a couple of things about McHenry that I likely shouldn't. He isn't going to howl too loud." He stopped then, and his features went somber. "You can pretty well figure out what happened and how they did it, if you piece a few things together. About two-thirty this morning, one of the hotel folks ran up to the deputy I had on your door, Miss Jessie. At least that's who he *said* he was. Told my man a couple of ranchers were killin' each other down on the fourth floor. The boy should've known better, but he knew Senator Hall was inside with you. 'Course, so did the killers. Anyway, a couple of hardcases hit him in the head and shoved him in a closet, and that was that."

103

"He's all right, isn't he?" Jessie asked anxiously.

"He is right now," Vail said sourly. "Won't be after I send him up in the mountains a couple of months, countin' Utes."

Marcus stood abruptly and faced Jessie. "Those killers are likely finished with me, but you're still on the list, damn it. I want you out of this, Jessie. Out of Denver, away from the whole mess!"

Jessie looked at him. "You think I should just walk away from it, is that it?"

"What I *think* is that I don't want you dead."

"I don't much care for the idea myself."

"Then, for God's sake," he blurted, "Let me get you out of this place—clear out of Denver!"

"All right," she said calmly. "I think you're absolutely right, Marcus."

"You—you do?" Marcus looked surprised.

"Yes. Remember what you told me last night? That Barbara Forsman had invited me to go along on that trek up to her place? I'm going to accept that invitation."

Marcus and Vail both exploded at once. Jessie shook her head and grinned. "Honestly, I don't *believe* you two. You've both done everything you can to convince me that Barbara and Lane are lily-white citizens."

"Jessie," Marcus said dryly, "some of the things you've told me make sense. I've already admitted that, haven't I? And if they *are* mixed up in this business, they sure as hell don't expect you to accept that invitation!"

Jessie gave him a long and thoughtful look. "You're wrong," she said finally. "Barbara Forsman knows me better than both of you do. She's guilty as sin, Marcus. She knows I don't believe a word she's told me about Lynnie, and she's expecting me to accept that invitation. She knows that's what I *have* to do now . . ."

The party headed west in the morning, following the well-traveled road out of Denver that a generation of miners had used to seek their fortunes. By noon they were past the broad prairie and into the foothills of the Rockies. After lunch, the way got steeper, as the trail wound up toward the Divide and the bald peaks of Berthoud Pass.

104

Jessie had to give Barbara credit. When she and Marcus showed up at Elaina's ranch, the lovely young woman rushed up to greet her like a sister. Hugging Jessie to her with tears in her eyes, she said she'd known from the start that they'd end up being friends.

"I owe you much more than an apology," she said contritely. "Since Lane was nearly killed, I've come to understand you better, Jessie. Whatever this monstrous thing's about, we'll see it through together!"

Jessie looked her straight in the eye, trying to conceal her distaste at the other woman's touch. "Yes," she said evenly, "we'll see it through together, Barbara."

Lane gave her a halfhearted greeting from his horse. The sniper's bullet had struck him in the shoulder, and his arm was bound to his chest in an elaborate sling. Marcus was still worried about that. If the Forsmans were involved, why had the sniper shot at *him?*

"I can't answer that," Jessie said bluntly. "Sorry, Marcus. As far as I'm concerned, that doesn't change a thing. Barbara's lying through her teeth. I know Lynnie was murdered, and I'm not buying fairy tales about morphine and evil English lovers. My God," she said fiercely, "she *knows* I don't believe it. She's desperate, and she's going to show her hand soon."

Marcus stared and shook his head in dismay. "Christ, I must have been out of my mind to bring you up here."

Before sunset, the Forsmans' hands rode ahead and made camp on the banks of Clear Creek. In the morning the party would climb to the Divide and trail down the western slope. Tables were set up, and a cookfire crackled in the middle of the camp. Lanterns hung from the trees, and the aromas of beans, corn on the cob, and roasting beef were in the air. For a moment the festive arrangements caught Jessie off guard. Barbara Forsman had created a charming picnic in the wilderness. She looked young, vibrant, flushed with excitement as she mingled with her guests. If she was a cold-blooded agent of the cartel, Jessie had to admit she was hiding it well.

Besides Marcus and herself and the Forsmans, there were three other couples on the trip. Jessie had seen them all at Elaina Culbertson's party, including Charles van Rijn and his young wife, Amanda. Amanda had sought her out and ridden along beside her, doing the best she could to keep tears from her eyes. "I reckon you know about me and Ki," she told Jessie. "At least I hope you do. Lord, Jessie, I cared for him a lot, and I want you to know it. I'm not ashamed of that."

Jessie's eyes misted at the girl's words. She leaned out in the saddle and grasped her hand. "Amanda, there's no reason you should be. Caring for a man like Ki is something special. He was a special kind of man."

"I don't know if I can—if I—oh, damn!" Amanda's face twisted in pain and she jerked her mount away and rode off by herself.

When supper was nearly over, riders appeared in the camp, and Jessie looked up to see Elaina Culbertson arrive in an open carriage, escorted by four hands from her ranch. She'd left after the main party, taking a slower, easier path. In spite of that, Jessie thought she looked drawn and pale, weary to the point of exhaustion. Barbara greeted her warmly, and Jessie caught the look in Elaina's eyes at the younger woman's embrace. *I was right the first time I saw those two together,* she told herself grimly. *Elaina's frightened to death, and Barbara Forsman's the cause!*

"I don't guess I can stay in your tent," Marcus said later. "Though I think it's a good idea, for more reasons than one."

"Oh?" Jessie said innocently. "And what's the *other* reason, Senator?"

Marcus glanced over his shoulder and kissed her quickly. "Hell, Jessie, if we did, this crowd's too refined even to notice. It's as though nothing ever happened at the Windsor, you know? And every damned one of them is dying to ask."

"Well, someone's looking out for us," Jessie said wryly. "Did you notice they very carefully set up our tents down in that little hollow, set off from the others? Whose cute idea do you suppose that was—our good friend Barbara's?"

Marcus's features suddenly grew sober. "Lane took me aside, Jessie, and told me Barbara finally shared her secret about Lynnie's past. Lane says he now thinks you're right, that there is some kind of conspiracy, and that maybe Lynnie was mixed up in it. He says he's certain it's an anarchist plot to overthrow the government by killing leaders in the Senate and people like

106

yourself, who control a lot of the wealth."

Jessie looked appalled. "Lord, Marcus, they must be getting worried—they're making stuff up as they go along!"

"I don't like it," Marcus said darkly. "I never should have brought you here at all."

Jessie rested her hand on his shoulder. "You can't stay in my tent tonight, Marcus. But if you decide you should check up on me later, I wouldn't mind at all. For both of the reasons you had in mind."

"Uh-huh. Don't think I won't," he told her firmly.

Jessie tried to stay awake, but exhaustion finally pulled her down into sleep. It seemed only minutes before a sound brought her up with a start. The fires had died, but the moon cast the shadows of trees on her tent, and created the dimmest sort of illumination inside.

"Marcus?" Jessie said softly. Her hand found the derringer at her thigh, and she brought the weapon up fast. "Marcus, damn it, if that's you, you'd better answer!"

Something moved quickly; its shadow brushed the canvas of her tent. Jessie sucked in a breath and shrank back.

"Marcus, answer me!" she said sharply.

"Jessie," a voice whispered out of the darkness. "Jessie, get out of there now!"

"What? Who are—"

"Get out, Jessie—*get out, for God's sake!*"

Jessie hesitated only a second. Bringing herself to a crouch, she bolted out of the tent in a roll, came to her feet, and ran. She gave no thought to a trap, a trick to get her into the open. The desperation and fear in that voice had been *real*...

A low branch tore at her hair. Jessie stumbled; strong hands reached out of nowhere and wrenched her to a stop. She screamed, then saw Marcus's face in the dark. He shouted, but his words were lost in a sudden thunder. Jessie knew the sound well, and it turned her blood to ice. As Marcus threw her to the ground and covered her body with his own, she saw the flash of hooves over her shoulder, the terrified whites of the horses' eyes. There were three dozen mounts in the camp, but it seemed to Jessie as if a thousand steel-hooved creatures pounded past her...

107

In seconds it was over. Dust clouded her sight, and the frightened mounts crashed through the trees down the hollow. Men began to shout, and lanterns winked in the dark. Marcus pulled Jessie shakily to her feet. She stared at the spot where their tents had stood only moments before. There was nothing there at all.

★

Chapter 12

"Christ, Aurochs—what's he doing in here? I don't need any of this right now. You should have gotten rid of him outside!"

"Maybe he knows somethin'. We can ask an' see..."

"You damned fool! If I'd wanted to talk to him, I wouldn't have told you to blow him up, now would I? God, how could you botch a thing like that? The girl—what's she got to do with him? Never mind, I'll get to her later. Give me an hour, then bring him upstairs. And Aurochs—leave him alone. Do you understand that? I can't talk to him if he's dead. What did you do to the girl?"

"I—I didn't do no bad stuff to her."

"You touched her, though, didn't you? You did something dirty."

"No, I—is truth, I—"

"Aurochs!"

"Uh, I touch her some. I don't do other thing!"

"You lie to me, you lout, and I'll cut that thing right off. Would you like that? Eh?"

"Don't—don't talk such thing. Aurochs don't like!"

"Bring him to me when I said. And don't touch him any-where, either..."

The voices swam through his head. They were there and then they were gone....Someone hit him and he screamed...He tried to remember where he was, what he'd heard....He couldn't think, couldn't remember....His head felt like a melon that had been left out in the sun....He brought himself to his knees and threw up....Big hands grabbed his shoulders, lifted him off the stone floor, and slammed him roughly into the chair...

Ki bit his lip to stifle the pain. Christ, everything hurt! The man had worked him over with his feet. He remembered some of it, and was grateful he'd missed the rest...

"Well, my friend. How do you feel now?"

Ki opened his eyes, focusing them dully on the man. He sat behind the big oak desk. His eyes looked like an owl's through the thick-lensed spectacles. He watched Ki with interest over the high arch of his fingers.

"I...know you," said Ki. The words came out like bubbles. He realized his lips were thick and bruised. "You're...saw you at Elaina Culbertson's...you're Sacchetti..."

The man gave him a satisfied grin. *"Doctor* Sacchetti. We say *Doctor* Sacchetti, young man."

"Where is she?" Ki rasped. "What've you done with her. Annie, she's—"

Sacchetti's smile faded. "Never speak to me like that. Never!"

"What have you done with her, you bastard! If you—"

Too late, Ki saw Sacchetti's slight nod. Fingers like steel squeezed the main nerve between his shoulder and his throat. His arms and legs jerked uncontrollably; his eyes were blind with pain, his scream a ragged cry that wouldn't stop.

Ki collapsed in his chair. Tears came, and he didn't try to stop them. It was better to let his body react to the pain, help the hurt die away. He made his decision without thinking. He was helpless; they could kill him, or cripple him so badly he'd never recover. If there was a chance in hell to stay alive and help Annie, he'd have to give himself to them completely.

"We understand each other now, don't we, Ki?"

"Yes....I understand..."

"'Yes, I understand, *sir*,'" Sacchetti corrected. "That's the proper way, isn't it?"

Ki looked up, forcing the words from his lips. "Yes . . . yes, *sir* . . ."

"Fine, fine." Sacchetti's head, perched on his scrawny neck, bobbed in approval. He stood, and nodded at the man behind Ki. "Bring him along, Aurochs. I'll be up on the other side." He grinned at Ki as if they were old friends. "Relax now," he said gently. "You won't be harmed again. I've decided to let you live for a while. Would you like that? You'd like to stay alive, wouldn't you?"

Sacchetti didn't wait for an answer. Still smiling, he bounded up from the desk and disappeared through a door at the far end of the room. The man called Aurochs dragged Ki roughly to his feet. Ki's stomach turned. The room reeled, and he struggled to keep his balance. If he fell, the bastard would kick him, and he wasn't sure he could take more of that.

Aurochs grabbed his arm and guided him roughly out the same door through which they'd entered. Past the door was a long, narrow hall, ending in a steep flight of rough granite stairs. Ki nearly groaned aloud when he saw them. God, did they really expect him to climb that? He was doing well to stay on his feet! Out of the corner of his eye, he saw a satisfied grin on the big man's face. Ki gritted his teeth, braced his hand against the hard stone wall, and took one shaky step up the stairs. *Keep smiling, you bastard*, he thought grimly. *I'm not dead yet . . .*

He shut the pain from his mind, put it out of his thoughts. His body moved grimly forward, but Ki was no longer there. His whole being was focused on Dr. Andrea Sacchetti. He remembered the stark figure next to Elaina Culbertson, the spindly little man dressed in black. Like an undertaker, Ki had thought at the time. A man no one would think about twice. He had started for Cheyenne to learn who the man was, what he might have to do with Lynnie's death. Instead, he had found Sacchetti himself, and now he knew Jessie was right; Sacchetti played some role in the cartel's scheme. And that meant the Forsmans were likely involved in the business as well. How, though? What were they all after? Ki had to laugh at himself. For all the good it would do him, he'd found the cartel's retreat.

He stopped before a solid wooden door; Aurochs passed him and swung it open. Ki blinked at the sudden brightness, and the big man shoved him roughly forward. Ki stumbled, caught himself, and tried to take in his surroundings. He was on a stone bridge, high above the ground. The bridge led from one high tower to another. Peering over the stone railing, he could see that the buildings ahead were separated from those behind him by a high rock wall. Except for the towers, neither section was visible from the other unless you stood on the bridge. Why? Ki wondered. Someone had obviously planned it that way. Two structures together, one hidden from the other.

"You move," grunted Aurochs. "No stop again!" The big man struck him on the back, and Ki quickly did as he was told.

Aurochs unlocked a door at the far end of the bridge and pushed Ki through. Dr. Sacchetti was there waiting, leaning against the wall. Behind him was a long stone porch, one side open to the sky. When Sacchetti saw Ki, he grinned and gave a sardonic bow of greeting.

"You went to a great deal of trouble to find us," he said gently. "I thought perhaps you'd like to see what we have. Marvelous, isn't it?" He spread his spindly arms to take in the high western slope of the Rockies. "Not quite what you expected? Eh?"

"I was following him," Ki said dully. "I didn't know where he was going."

Sacchetti stepped closer and gave him a thoughtful frown. "And before that, Ki, just where were you headed on that train? I'm curious about that."

Ki could feel Aurochs looming behind him. "Cheyenne," he answered evenly. "I was going to Cheyenne."

"And what for, may I ask?"

"Jessica Starbuck sent me."

Irritation touched the man's gaunt features. "Don't make me *ask* you things, young man."

"She—sent me there to get help." Ki paused, long enough to let Sacchetti know he didn't want to answer the question. "She asked me to hire some people and bring them back. Some men who could help."

112

Sacchetti raised a brow. "Gunmen, you mean? She could have done that in Denver."

"No. Too much was happening there. She didn't trust anyone in Denver."

Sacchetti licked his lips. "And the girl was traveling with you."

He started to say yes, but he caught the look of cunning behind the owlish glasses. Sacchetti knew that was a lie. "No. I know her...but I don't know what she was doing on the train. That's the truth."

"Oh, I know it is, Ki." Sacchetti gave him a broad grin. "Miss McCullough has been kind enough to, ah, talk to me quite freely."

"Is Annie all right?" Ki blurted. "You haven't—"

"Aurochs!" snapped Sacchetti.

Aurochs gripped his shoulders in two big hands and started to squeeze. Ki gasped, and Sacchetti raised a hand. "The girl is not a subject for discussion. Did you forget that, Ki?"

Ki swallowed his anger. "Yes. Yes, sir. I forgot."

"Good, good!" Ki's words seemed to please him immensely. "Come now, I have something to show you."

The covered balcony circled the building over a broad paved courtyard. A few steps farther on, Sacchetti stopped and motioned Ki to him. Ki pressed his hands on the railing and looked below. At first he simply stared, trying to comprehend what he was seeing. Then he blinked his eyes to clear them, as if his mind had played some trick on his vision. Sacchetti laughed at his confusion, but Ki hardly heard him. He was struck dumb where he stood, as if he'd climbed a rise in the desert and seen a broad blue ocean at his feet. It was there—but it simply couldn't be!

The shaded courtyard was three stories below. Only it wasn't in the wilds of Colorado, it was a thousand miles away—New Orleans, maybe, or a boulevard in Paris. Round tables with white linen cloths were clustered together like a sidewalk cafe. Waiters scurried about carrying trays of colorful drinks, delicate cups of coffee, and small pastries.

The only customers were women; Ki counted seventeen young girls. They lounged about the tables, sparkling glasses

113

in their white-gloved hands, or chatted in small groups about the courtyard. All were dressed in well-cut, fashionable gowns—dresses chosen to complement the color of their hair, the soft tones of their eyes. There were amber-haired girls with flesh like ivory and cream; raven-haired beauties with eyes like smoke; slim, golden-tressed girls with flashing blue eyes and skin like honey. No two were alike, yet all had one thing in common; they were sensuous, wildly desirable women who could step into a room anywhere in the world and capture the eyes of every man there. Ki had seen only a handful like them in his life. It wasn't just their beauty that set them apart; it was something in their eyes, the way they held their bodies. They were as cold and out-of-reach as a perfect cut gem. Yet in the blink of an eye they were bitches in heat. With one smoldering look they could promise a man everything he wanted...

Sacchetti's soft laughter brought him up with a start. "Lovely, aren't they? Charming creatures. Come along, young man. There's still more to see."

Ki stood his ground. "What the hell's going on here?" he asked shortly. "What are you doing to those girls?"

Sacchetti looked amused. "Don't you know? Really? I'm not *doing* anything to them, my friend. Except teaching them, of course. Teaching them all the little things they need to know."

Ki frowned. "Teaching them *what?*"

Sacchetti's smile faded. "I don't much care for your tone of voice. I've warned you about that, haven't I?"

"What are you doing, goddamn it!" raged Ki. "Why are those—"

"Aurochs!"

Ki knew it was coming, but couldn't stop it. His body was too slow, too sluggish to respond. The first blow took him in the small of the back and sent him sprawling. The second caught him squarely in the ribs and loosened a cry from his lips. Then Aurochs stepped in close and started working on him with his boots. Ki felt nothing at all after that...

The cell was small, and stank like a sewer.

He could crawl about on his knees, but there was no room

114

to stand. Stretching out on the cold stone floor, he peered up at the small iron grating overhead. The grating let a little fresh air into his cell, but hardly any light. A dull ache throbbed through his body, but Ki scarcely knew it was there. After a certain amount of pain, the feeling had simply gone.

His mind was still reeling from what he'd seen. The answer was there, somewhere at the edge of his thoughts.

Beautiful women with bold, flashing eyes... women who smelled of musk and the raw heat of lust... women who could draw a man into their arms, whisper promises that would—

Promises. Promises that would do *what?* The thought suddenly struck him and turned him cold. And with the thought came an image—ice-blue eyes, lips full and soft, and a face like an angel. Barbara. Barbara Forsman. Good God, of course—*she was one of them, cut from the same cloth!* He knew in an instant that it was true. Jessie had sensed it from the start, seen something in her eyes. Ki was dead certain now—Barbara had once stood there in that very same courtyard, smiling, touching a glass to her lovely mouth.

I'm teaching them... teaching them all the little things they need to know...

Sacchetti's words came back with new meaning. Christ, was that the man's job, taking young girls and turning them into deadly weapons? Ki didn't doubt it for a minute. The cartel did everything in its power to put its own people in high places. And a woman like Barbara, or one of the others—who could get closer to the wealthy head of a railroad, a rich eastern broker, or even a United States senator?

The enormity of the scheme overwhelmed him. Lane Forsman—Lord, and how many others already? Forsman was a perfect target, a power in his state, a man who had a hand in shaping the West. He'd be a real catch for the cartel, though Ki doubted that Barbara had needed to work her wiles on such a man. Forsman's greed for power showed in his eyes. More than likely, he'd come to the cartel willingly, happy to have a prize like Barbara on his arm.

Marcus Hall, though—he was another story altogether. Totally different from Forsman, he was a man who couldn't be bought or corrupted. They'd have to be careful with Marcus.

He was a man destined to go right to the top: an advisor to the President, a member of the Cabinet, maybe even the highest office itself . . .

Ki shuddered at the thought. That had been the cartel's purpose for Lynnie, to marry Marcus and rise with him. A perfect, loving woman who could charm her husband's friends, and learn things few other women would ever know. And suppose Marcus did reach the top, what more could the cartel ask? *If the First Lady was one of their own, the country itself would be in their pocket!*

Only something had happened, Ki thought to himself. Something went wrong with Sacchetti's prize pupil, and he killed her. Did Lynnie decide that she wasn't like the others, that she didn't *want* the awesome power the cartel could grant a beautiful woman?

Ki sighed and sank back to the cold stone floor. What the hell difference did it make what he knew and what he didn't? Unless he could get himself out of the mess he was in, he was certainly as good as dead—and so was Annie McCullough. Aurochs was determined to kill him. Maybe next time, Sacchetti wouldn't bother to stop him . . .

"Ki? Ki, are you down there?"

"Huh?" Ki started, pulled himself up and grasped the thick iron grating. "Annie! My God, is that you?"

"Hush," she warned him, "don't talk any louder." Her fingers touched the spaces between the cold metal bars. "I can't stay, Ki, I—Oh, Lord, I thought you were dead!"

"Annie—Annie, are you all right? They haven't hurt you?"

"I'm all right, Ki. Just scared to death. They—they've got me working in the kitchen. This drain's in a kind of storeroom close by. One of the servants said they were keeping someone down here, and I figured it might be you. Oh, Ki, I know what they're doing in this place. I found out!"

"Yes, I know too, Annie. Listen, can you get me a file, a knife, anything? A piece of metal, whatever you can find."

"I'll try—only I don't know when I can get back down here. They watch us real closely. Ki, I've got to tell you this quick. A rider came in from somewhere and went upstairs, and then came down here to get something to eat. He'd been talking

116

to that awful Dr. Sacchetti, and he was laughing about what Sacchetti said."

Annie stopped, and Ki leaned closer to the grating. "What, Annie? What is it?"

"Jessie's coming," she blurted. "Jessie's coming here."

"*What!*" Ki's stomach tightened in a knot. "Annie, what the hell are you saying?"

Annie's voice caught. "Ki, the rider said—it doesn't make sense now, but he said Sacchetti thought it was funny because now he wouldn't have to—have to let the other man kill you. *Now he'd just let Jessica Starbuck do it herself!*"

"Let Jessie kill me? Annie, that's crazy. She— Annie? *Annie!*"

Her fingers pulled away. He clutched at the iron grille a long time, but she was gone.

★

Chapter 13

Marcus stalked angrily toward the glowing lanterns, slapping dust from his denims. Jessie saw the look in his eyes and knew there was no use trying to stop him. A wrangler rushed up with his rifle, and stared at Marcus and the ruined ground behind him. Marcus swept him aside and kept going. He spotted Lane Forsman coming out of his tent, stuffing his shirttail in his trousers. Marcus grabbed a handful of collar and turned him roughly around.

"Goddammit," he roared, "we nearly got killed down there! What's going on here, Lane?"

"J-Jesus, Hall!" Lane looked stricken, his face as pale as dough.

"Answer me, you bastard!" Marcus raised his fist, and Lane shrank back.

"Marcus, stop it!" screamed Barbara. She grabbed his arm tightly with both hands, and hung on. Marcus turned, stared as if he'd never seen her before, blinked at Lane, and threw him roughly away.

Lane caught himself and stood up straight. "Hell, man, what was that all about?"

Marcus pointed a trembling hand down toward the hollow, and the remains of the ruined tents.

Barbara stared past him. Suddenly, understanding crossed her features. "Lord God!" She brought a hand to her face, saw Jessie, and started toward her. Something in Jessie's eyes stopped her, and she stayed where she was. "Are you—are you all right, Jessie? This is simply *awful!*"

"Yes, it is, isn't it?" Jessie said dryly. Marcus was still glaring at Lane, and Jessie took a step toward him. "Marcus, this isn't going to help. May I borrow that lantern, Barbara?" She took the light without waiting for an answer. "Why don't we all go and take a look? I'd kind of like to see how those horses got loose."

"Jessie's absolutely right," Barbara said suddenly. "Stay here, Lane. You don't need to come." Wrapping her robe tightly about her, she guided Marcus deftly away from Lane, toward the clearing. Several members of the party had come sleepily out of their tents, and Barbara shot them a charming smile. "Everything's all right now. We're terribly sorry for all the commotion. Charlie, Jake!" she called sharply. "Get over here, and bring some more light. I want to talk to you two." She turned then, and moved off up the hill, giving the cowhands hell as she walked.

Jessie stared after her, hands on her hips. "Damn that woman!" she said furiously. With a word and a smile, Barbara had effectively pulled Jessie's fuse. Now it looked as if checking out the horses had been her idea from the beginning . . .

Dawn was reddening the sky by the time the hands rounded up the last stray. The cooks provided a first-class breakfast, and Barbara brought Jessie and Marcus a section of rope that she said had snapped when something spooked the mounts. A wolf, one of the hands figured; he'd heard them in the distance before dark.

"Doesn't matter what it was," she said tightly. "I've fired the men responsible for the horses. There is no excuse for a thing like that." Her face softened, and she gave Marcus and Jessie a lovely smile. "I'm sorry. I'd give anything if this hadn't

120

happened." Turning on her heel, she stalked back to the cookfire. Like Jessie, she was dressed in skintight denims. Long blond hair fell to a slim little waist, and her bottom twitched provocatively as she walked.

"All right, damn it." Jessie poked Marcus in the ribs. "Just put your eyes back in your head, friend. That fine-looking lady tried to turn you into hamburger this morning, remember?"

Marcus gave her a sheepish grin. "I remember, but I keep forgetting."

"Well, don't," Jessie snapped. She sighed and sipped her coffee. "Wolves, huh? With how many legs?" She shuddered, in spite of the morning sun. "That woman's got all the warm feeling of a snake, Marcus. And damn her—she's the best looking female I ever saw." Marcus started to speak, and Jessie raised a finger in warning. "You agree with me, fellow, and you are in big, big trouble!"

The long summer day was nearly gone when the party crossed the high Berthoud Pass and angled down the western slope of the Rockies. Jessie was almost certain Barbara wouldn't try anything again until they reached their destination, but Marcus refused to leave her side.

"That's just an excuse," said Jessie with a grin. "You figure if I let you in my tent, you'll charm me out of my clothes and have your way with me again."

"The thought had crossed my mind," he admitted.

"Huh! So who's guarding me from *you?*"

"Do you need someone?"

"Well, I didn't the last time."

"Then we don't have a thing to worry about, do we?"

"No," Jessie said cheerily, "no one but Lane and Barbara and God knows what kind of assassins they've got lurking in the woods." Her smile faded, and she gave him a sober look. "What's going to happen? When we get to their place, I mean. I know you're right, and it was a damn fool thing to come up here, but Marcus, I've turned all the rocks over and let the bugs crawl out. She can't just clobber us both with an ax in front of the whole party, you know? Folks like Billy Vail know where we are. It'd be downright insane to try anything else!"

"I wouldn't have bet they'd have the nerve to do what they

121

did—then smile and say they're sorry." He gripped her arm and gave her a long, hard look. "Jessie, let me get you out of here in the morning. We can lag back when the group gets going, and ride south. There are a couple of settlements not far away. We don't even have to cross the Divide."

Jessie smiled wearily. "Thanks, Marcus. We're in it now, though, and I guess we'd better stay in." She didn't say the words; his eyes told her he already knew. There was no guarantee that Barbara Forsman would let them get very far if they tried . . .

The country west of the Divide was some of the prettiest Jessie had ever seen. One of the riders told her the ranch was some thirty miles to the north—not too far, but it would take most of the day to cross the thick forests and rolling hills. By nine in the morning, the party was winding its way through narrow green valleys and rushing mountain streams. Pines stood straight and tall against the Rockies. Grasses and golden flowers dotted the white aspen slopes, and the land was full of elk and deer.

Jessie had found no chance at all to talk to Elaina Culbertson. The older woman and her riders were usually far behind the main party. That made a casual meeting hard to manage, and Jessie didn't want to risk putting the woman in danger. *When we get to the ranch,* she promised herself firmly, *there'll be a chance then—and if there's not, I'll damn sure make one. I have to talk to Elaina, find out what she knows!*

More than once, Jessie had started to tell Marcus that she knew who'd warned her the night of the stampede. The realization had dawned on her as she and Marcus had stood staring at their demolished tents; it had been Elaina Culbertson's voice whispering urgently in the night outside her tent. For some reason, though, each time she had begun to reveal this information to Marcus, something held her back.

He was quieter and more withdrawn with every mile. She caught him watching Lane Forsman, his eyes following every move the man made. She realized he was a bomb simply waiting to go off, and she wasn't about to light a match close by.

The trail got easier by late afternoon, as the hills gentled out and broad valleys appeared to the east. Topping a high rise, Jessie could see rolling grassland stretching west and far to the north.

"Charlie says the ranch is just ahead and to the right," Amanda said as she reined in beside Jessie. "Back toward the Rockies."

"Have you been there before?"

"No. Charlie has, though. He says Lane Forsman likes to say the ranch is a monument to his father—you know, old H. R. Forsman, who had a real big spread in Texas. He made a fortune moving cattle up north. Only Charlie thinks it's Lane's tribute to himself. I sure wouldn't doubt it—I can't *stand* that man. You've heard about the place, haven't you?"

"No," Jessie said curiously. "it's just a ranch, isn't it?"

Amanda rolled her eyes. "Not from what Charlie says. More like a damn castle or something. With towers and the whole works. Sticking right out of a big granite mesa. Built it when he and Barbara got married, and—" Amanda stopped, glanced over her shoulder, then looked hard at Jessie. "Ki asked me about the Forsmans. I guess you know that. Mostly about Barbara, and what she had to do with your friend Lynnie. Jessie, I don't know what's going on here, but I was Ki's friend, and I'm yours too. Remember that, will you?"

"I will," Jessie said warmly. "And thank you, Amanda."

An hour before sunset, outriders from the Forsman spread rode through the trees to greet the party. Past the next hill, the land opened up to a broad valley stretching as far as the eye could see. Vast herds of cattle dotted the plains, and one of the guests told Marcus they were now on Forsman land. "Goes on forever," the man grinned. "Lane's got more goddamn cows than he can count, and all of 'em prime beef."

Beyond the great herds, a thunderhead swept over the mountains from the north. Lightning forked the ground, and the light turned a strange lemon-yellow. The party turned west away from the storm, back toward the foothills of the Rockies. Half an hour later, Jessie rode her horse through the trees got her first look at the Forsman retreat.

"Good Lord!" she gasped, staring at the high s "If that's a ranch house, Marcus, we've been do in Texas!"

Marcus studied the twin stone towers, the sheer rock wall of the mesa. "I don't like this at all, Jessie. Damn, that place looks like a prison! If we ride into that thing—"

Jessie touched his shoulder. "We'll handle it as it comes, Marcus. If she tries anything, we'll be ready."

"Like last time, right?"

Jessie forced a grin. "Sorry. Looks like you're going to have to keep sleeping with me, friend. I wouldn't have it any other way."

"*You* sleep," growled Marcus. "I think I'm staying awake."

There was only one way up the steep side of the ridge, a path that wound its way around the high granite spine like a snake. The road was wide enough for a wagon, but no wider. At the top, a thick timbered gate creaked open to let them in—then slammed shut ominously behind them. The gate faced the first of the two towers, past a broad open courtyard paved in stone. The first thing the Forsmans' guests saw was a long wooden table covered in linen. The table groaned with fine food and drink of every description—steaming platters of beef, chicken, quail, sausage, elk and venison steaks, and hot breads. At intervals along the table were bottles of champagne nestled in ice-filled silver buckets. The weary travelers applauded Lane and Barbara, and let waiting hands take their horses.

Lane beamed, and wandered among his guests. "This here's just to get you back on your feet," he told them. "We'll have a real sit-down supper about nine."

To Jessie's surprise, Lane walked straight up to Marcus and stuck out his hand. "I'm sorry you and me got crosswise back there," he said sincerely. "You're welcome here, Marcus, and you too, Jessie. I mean that, damn it."

Marcus took his hand and muttered his thanks, but Lane had gotten started and wouldn't stop. "I want to talk to you two later. Both of you. Whoever's behind this business is trying to start bad feelings between us, and that isn't going to work. All right?"

"Fine," Marcus said flatly. "I'd like nothing better than the chance to talk to you, Lane."

"Good, good!" Lane pumped his hand again and winked at ˈsie. "Now you two enjoy yourselves." He walked off quickly, calling out to a Denver banker and his wife.

"Lord!" Jessie shook her head in wonder. "The man's got gall, you've got to hand him that."

"I hope he means that about having a little talk. If I ever get that son of a bitch alone, I'll get some answers."

"Marcus, you'll do nothing of the sort," Jessie said with alarm. "You won't learn a thing by breaking Lane Forsman's jaw. Although I wouldn't mind a chance at that myself!"

Jessie chatted with Amanda, and tried to keep an eye on Barbara, who was, as ever, the perfect hostess, making certain every guest had plenty to eat and a full glass of champagne. Finally she mounted the first few steps leading into the tower and clapped her hands.

"Ladies and gentlemen, may I have your attention a minute, please? If you'll all go inside, we'll show you to your rooms. Your baggage is already there, and you'll all be staying on the second floor of the building, right behind the tower. We've assigned a personal servant to each couple—he'll be close by whenever you need him during your stay, so don't hesitate to just ask for whatever you want. See you at supper, and welcome to our home!"

The guests applauded, and followed her inside. Barbara stood next to a line of tall, solidly built men in black shirts and pressed trousers. "Oh, Marcus and Jessie, there you are," Barbara smiled. "Here are your keys—you're in seven and eight; they're marvelous rooms and I know you'll be comfortable."

"Thanks," Jessie said warily. "I'm sure we will."

Barbara touched the sleeve of an enormous man at her side. Jessie looked up and stared. He was as ugly as sin, but a broad smile creased his features. "I'm giving you one of my very best men. Doesn't speak much English, but he's a jewel. Just ask for anything you need."

The man bowed his bulletlike head on his thick bull neck and looked straight at Jessie. "At your service, lady," he said haltingly. "I am name Aurochs. You want somethin' I be plenty close, yes?"

★

Chapter 14

Ki floated up into wakefulness, groaned, and rubbed grit out of his eyes. He hurt like hell all over. His mouth was dry, and there was a dull ache in his belly. In spite of the chill air of his cell, his skin was flushed with fever. He could smell the sour odor of his sweat and knew what it meant. If he didn't get out soon, sickness would sap his strength. It would weaken his body and go to work on his mind, drain his will and leave him as helpless as a child.

Gritting his teeth, he pulled himself up in the darkness, and found the iron grating with his fingers. How long had he slept? An hour, two hours? He knew there was no way to tell, that time wasn't the same in the dark. Maybe Annie had left a few minutes ago—or maybe the day before.

Jessie! He suddenly remembered, and stared into the dark. Could Annie be right about that? Was she a prisoner h
He shook his head to clear the cobwebs away. Anni
something else about Jessie . . . she was going to
didn't make sense, but then, what the hell did?

127

After a moment, he left the iron grille and crawled to the other end of the cell. He knew the dimensions by heart. Three feet high and nearly three wide—and a little over seven feet long. The door was solid iron, just wide enough for a man's shoulders. There was a peephole at the top. For a while he had crouched there, looking out, but there was really nothing to see. A hall with wet stone walls, and the dim glow of a lantern somewhere out of sight. There were two other cells like his own, directly across the corridor. If anyone was inside, they'd never answered his call. As far as Ki knew, no one had even come to look at him since Aurochs had shoved him inside. They certainly hadn't brought food or water.

He leaned against the door, watching pale light on the outside wall. A rat scurried down the hall, stopping to sniff the ground and the cells across the way. It turned, sat up on it haunches, and looked boldly at Ki, its red eyes gleaming. Ki tapped on the door and sent it scuttling away.

His body was cramping fast, and he moved from the door to stretch out. Closing his eyes, he pillowed his head on his arms, took a deep breath, and let it out slowly. An image kept worrying the edge of his mind. It was the scene he'd watched moments before—the hall, the dim light, the rat, and the cells across the way. There was something there, something that—

Ki suddenly sat up straight and crawled painfully back to the door. Pressing his cheek to the cold metal, he peered across the hall once more. *The other doors, that was it!* His heart beat quickened. There was no lock on any of the cells across the way. And that meant there was likely none on his door, either. There was a flat bar, hinged to the door itself. To secure the door, the bar was simply dropped behind a flat metal lip attached to the jamb. It was the way you kept horses in a stall— the simplest lock in the world, and as good as a St. Louis vault if you couldn't reach the bar.

Ki studied the bars on the doors across the way, then sat back and started tearing at his denims. His trousers were all they'd left him, so they'd have to do. The fabric was tough, but one leg was frayed enough to let him rip it up to the knee.

After a while he had several long strips. Knotting them together, he tied a loop in one end and crawled back to the door. If his was like the others, the lock bar was some nine

128

inches below the peephole, and three inches over. He'd have to lower the cloth loop, swing it out, and catch the end of the bar.

It was a slow, painstaking operation. The peephole was only a slit; he could barely push the tips of his fingers outside to swing the loop, and could only guess where the end of the bar might be. His hands cramped; sweat stung his eyes. Every few moments he had to stop and let his body quit shaking. He had no idea how many hours crawled by. Just a few tries more . . . a few more times, and the loop had to—

Ki froze. The cloth suddenly caught. Biting his tongue, he lifted the loop slowly, praying it wouldn't slip off, as it had a hundred times before. He felt the weight of the bar and knew he had it. Raising it another slow inch, he closed his eyes and pressed the door firmly with his hand. The door swung open.

Ki stared, unable to believe he was free . . .

It was a luxury simply to stand up straight. He flexed his arms and legs and moved quickly down the hall. There was a wooden door at the end. If the damn thing was locked . . . he pulled it back slowly and breathed a sigh of relief. Moving inside, he leaned against the wall to get his bearings. There were stairs a few yards away. As he'd guessed, he was still underground, below the level of the courtyard. He'd been in bad shape when Aurochs dragged him back to the cell, but he was certain they hadn't crossed back over the bridge.

Ki frowned. Annie had said the grating was in a storeroom off the kitchen. He knew the retreat was divided into a public and a very private half, beyond the bridge and the wall—the half where the cartel kept its harem of lovely ladies. Did that mean there were *two* kitchens, then? There didn't have to be— not if Aurochs had carried him underground *below* the court- yard, back to the other side. He hoped that was so. If it was, he could get into the kitchen, steal some food and water, and think about how to get to Annie and Jessie.

At the top of the stairs, one corridor led straight ahead, while another twisted off to the left. He remembered the one to the left and passed it by. Aurochs had dragged him over its rough stone paving after Ki's "tour" with Dr. Sacchetti. Straight ahead, then. If his sense of direction was working, he was right above his old cell. A moment later, the arched stone alcoves on either side of the hall told him he was right. Two were empty, but the others were piled high with crates and barrels, as well as sacks of potatoes, onions, and flour. Ki tore a raw potato out of a sack and wolfed it down. In the center of each storage area, a small iron grille was set in the floor, which meant the kitchen was nearby, likely just—

Ki dropped quickly behind a pile of barrels and boxes. A man laughed only a few yards away, and a girl answered. In a moment they were gone, carrying a sack between them. Ki raised himself cautiously and followed them with his eyes. Down the hall and to the right. He waited a moment, then followed. Halfway down the hall, he stopped. There was a barrel against the wall, and resting on its top was the prettiest sight he'd ever seen—a sturdy steel crowbar, a good three feet long. He hefted it in his fist and grinned. His flesh was hot with fever, but he felt a hell of a lot better already...

Staying close to the wall, he risked a look around the edge of the door. The kitchen was enormous, as large as a fair-sized cabin. The smells almost drove Ki mad. Steam rose to the vaulted stone ceiling from half a dozen stoves. Cooks yelled at each other, and waiters scurried about with heavy trays. At the far end of the kitchen, four girls in white caps and aprons were scrubbing pots and dishes. Ki spotted Annie at once; she was the only one of the four who weighed under two hundred pounds.

Someone was bound to stop him in seconds. A man dressed in torn denims and no shirt didn't belong. Several small kegs were lined up beside the door, along with a stepladder, a bucket, and a mop. Ki's eyes fell on a large wicker basket of soiled laundry. With a quick look in the kitchen, he slid past the door, stashed his crowbar in the basket, lifted it up in front of his face, and made his way across the room. No one even turned to look his way.

He stopped beside Annie; she was bent over the basin, her hands covered in suds.

"Annie," he said softly, "if you scream right now, we're both dead. Get out of here *now,* and I'll follow. Don't hurry, just do it."

130

Annie went stiff. Without turning, she nodded her head and wiped her hands clean. Walking past Ki, she spoke to one of the cooks, who absently waved her aside. Ki followed as she crossed the room and disappeared through a low door.

He dropped the basket and she threw herself at him, tears streaming down her face. "Oh, God, Ki—I never expected to see you again. I couldn't get back and— What happened? How'd you get out?"

Ki kissed her quickly and held her away, glancing nervously over his shoulder. "I'll explain later," he told her. "Annie, where are we? Right now?"

Annie wiped her face. "This corridor goes to the maids' quarters—the girls who work in the kitchen. Lord, nobody's exactly hired help in this place. Everybody's like me—you just work and get fed, and if you try to get away—"

"All right. Now, what else is up there? Where can you go besides the maids' rooms? An outside door, a window . . ."

Annie shook her head. "Windows. But they're either barred or too small to get through." Her eyes went wide with fear. "Ki, those men in black, like the ones who caught me on the train—they're all over the place. If they catch us—"

"They're not going to catch us," he assured her. "Come on. We'll find a way." Annie sighed and climbed the stairs. Ki retrieved his crowbar and followed. The rooms were no more than cubicles with straw mattresses and blankets. He saw that Annie was right about the windows. The ones that were large enough were barred.

"One of the guards will be up to check on me," Annie warned. "I was supposed to be going to the bathroom. The head cook'll turn me in—they get extra privileges for things like that."

Ki wasn't listening. He was testing the bars on a hall window. The second and third bar were loose in their mortar base. He grinned and started chipping away with the crowbar. Annie looked appalled. "What are we going to do even if you can get us out? Ki, there's no place to go!"

"We'll worry about that when it happens," he told her. "You said Jessie was coming, Annie. Is that true? Do you know where she is?"

Annie shook her head. "I told you all I knew. But I do

know the Forsmans are here now. This is *their* place, there's no question about that. They're having a big dinner or something right now. That's why everyone's busy in the kitchen. You said you knew about the girls, didn't you?"

"Yes," Ki said grimly. "I got the grand tour with Dr. Sacchetti. Have you seen the other side?"

"No. I know about it—but none of the help will say much. They're all too scared. If you ever—" Annie stopped, staring at Ki in alarm. "Oh, Lord, you're sick. You're sweating all over!" She touched his head and her eyes went wide. "Ki, you are burning up with fever!"

"I know, Annie," he said calmly. "I am also hungry and I hurt all over. Unfortunately, we don't have time to worry about that." Wiping his brow, he put down the crowbar and grasped the bars of the window in his hands. One came loose in his fist and he handed it to Annie. The other was more firmly embedded, but he managed to bend it aside at a slight angle.

"That ought to be enough," he told her. Peering out, he studied the area quickly, then ducked back inside. "We're in luck. There are a couple of stubs of timber jutting out of the stone wall. Probably part of the flooring in here. We can hang on those and drop into the courtyard. It's only one story down." Annie started to protest, but Ki simply lifted her under her arms and sat her on the window. She had no place to go but out. Ki followed, made sure she was all right, then grabbed the wooden holds and dropped to the ground. Annie seemed to hang in midair forever, but finally let go. Ki broke her fall, and nearly passed out from the effort.

The courtyard was dark; he was thankful that low clouds masked the moon. Bright light came from a window far to the left. From the laughter and the smell of good food, he guessed it was the main dining room. Grasping Annie's hand, he worked his way quickly around the base of the tower. The outside wall of the retreat was a good twenty feet high. Ki ignored it. There was no way in the world he could scale it in his condition, without help or a rope.

Peering around the tower, he could see the timbered gate that must lead out of the retreat. There was a dim lantern on either side, another on a pole at the top of the wall. As he watched, someone struck a match and lit a smoke, and he saw the two men in shadow.

"Stay here," he told Annie. "Don't move until I come back for you, all right?"

"Ki!" She clutched his arm in an iron grip. "Ki, what are you going to do?"

He loosened her fingers and moved away from the tower, keeping low in shadow. The large front door was set back in darkness, half a dozen stone steps above the courtyard. Ki crouched and took a breath. Bending to the ground, he felt about with his fingers and found two loose rocks the size of marbles. He studied the guards at the gate for a moment, then tossed one of the stones against the wall, twenty yards to the right. The men came instantly alert. Ki heard the metallic double click as one of the guards levered a round into his rifle.

The first stayed at his post while the other ran hurriedly down the wall. The guard at the gate watched his companion, and Ki darted from cover. His samurai training had taught him to move like a shadow. He was four feet behind the man at the gate when the guard spun around and brought up his rifle. Ki swung the crowbar with both hands. It hit the man in the chest, over the heart. Ki grabbed the rifle before it fell, caught the limp body, and eased it to the ground. Before the other guard started back, Ki was dressed in his victim's black shirt, carrying his Winchester.

The man walked toward him. "Nothing down there. You see anything?"

Ki muttered an answer and kept his head low.

"Klaus? What is—" The man backed off and brought up his weapon. Ki knew he'd never quiet him in time, and pulled the trigger. The harsh explosion rolled around the courtyard like thunder.

"Annie!" Ki shouted. "Get over here fast!" Annie broke from shadow. Ki dropped his rifle and started pulling on the heavy wooden bar that held the gate. His efforts cost him dearly. His eyes were going blurry and his legs felt like water. He cursed his body for failing, and tugged at the bar.

Annie screamed. Ki turned and saw the door to the tower burst open. Light spilled over the courtyard, catching Annie as she raced toward him.

"Get down!" he shouted. Going to his belly, he grabbed up the Winchester as several guns fired and bullets slammed into the gate at his back. Black-suited men poured down the steps.

Ki shook his eyes to clear them. He picked out a running figure, and squeezed the trigger. A man cursed, threw down his Colt, and folded. Another staggered and fell, with a bullet in his belly. The other men froze, then turned and ran for the door, suddenly aware that they were targets against the light. Ki emptied the rifle after them, sending another man sprawling. Annie got to her feet and stumbled toward him. Fire blossomed from the far corner of the tower, striking sparks from the stone paving. Grabbing up the second rifle, Ki rolled and came to his haunches, away from the lanterns by the gate, and fired a quick volley into shadow. A gunman howled, and pulled himself to cover.

For a brief moment the courtyard was empty. Annie reached his side and Ki swept her behind him. He knew it was too late, they'd never make it now. At another time he would have chanced the timbered gate, climbed the damn thing, and carried Annie over with him. Now the fever was burning him up, bringing him to the ground.

"I want you to go," he told her tightly. "Behind me. Run close to the wall and keep going."

"No!" Annie shook her head fearfully. "No, Ki, I won't!"

"Do it!" He gripped her shoulders hard, and threw her roughly away. "Get out of here, Annie—now!"

He moved along the wall without looking back. He could see them again, bunched up around the tower. Boot heels echoed off stone in another direction. They had him flanked, then. No place to go. Nowhere to run. *Fine—end it right here*, he thought calmly. *It's as good a place as any . . .*

A gunman broke from cover by the tower. Ki snapped off a shot and took off running. Fire brightened the courtyard. Lead chipped stone at his heels. Ki rolled and came to his feet. Shots flashed out of the night from two directions. Ki fired blindly, sweeping the rifle from left to right. Too late, he sensed the presence above him, and jerked aside as shadows dropped from the wall. Something slammed his back and pulled him down. Ki struck out, chopping with the edge of his hand. A man cursed and spat blood. Ki kicked hard and sent another gunman sprawling.

Suddenly he was alone. They stood in a circle around him, weapons at the ready. He heard Annie's stifled cry nearby, but there was nothing he could do.

134

Dr. Sacchetti pushed the others aside, looked at Ki, and glanced over his shoulder. "Get him out of here," he snapped angrily. "Now! I want this courtyard completely cleared!"

Two men bent to take his shoulders, while another leveled a Colt.

"*No!*" An arm as big as a tree limb reached down and swept the two men aside. Aurochs loomed over Ki, his face twisted with rage. "This one mine. You say this. I get to kill!"

"No," Sacchetti said tightly, "he is *not* yours. I told you that before."

"Mine," Aurochs said between his teeth. "I kill him." A vicious growl began in the big man's throat. He took a threatening step toward Sacchetti, fists trembling at his sides. Sacchetti stood his ground. For a moment, Ki was certain Aurochs would lift the little man and take off his head. But instead, he turned suddenly and stalked across the yard into the darkness.

★

Chapter 15

Lane Forsman stood to make a toast, stumbled, and nearly fell over backwards in his chair. The guests laughed, and Forsman tried again. This time, Barbara scolded him and made him sit down. Lane gave up and focused his attention on Amanda van Rijn's plunging neckline across the table. Amanda gave him a hard, frosty look, and Lane turned to the lady on his left. She was in her mid-sixties and as skinny as a rail. Lane no longer seemed to care, and the lady was delighted.

"My God," moaned Jessie, "this is a bad dream, Marcus. We're going to wake up and be somewhere else."

"Just take it easy," he told her. His hand found hers under the table. "Supper can't last forever."

"Marcus, look!" Jessie cut him off and leaned close. "There's Elaina and—Lord, it's Dr. Sacchetti. He's here too. I don't guess I should be surprised."

Lane and Barbara turned to greet Elaina. The older woman gave them a weary smile, and Sacchetti helped her to a chair. Jessie thought she looked as pale as death. Her flesh was drawn,

137

and her eyes were mirrors of pain. It was only the second time she'd really seen Sacchetti—she'd caught just a glimpse of him at Elaina's party. She was shocked to find that the image she'd formed in her mind was nothing at all like the man himself. He was a small, fragile creature who looked more like someone's clerk than like a prominent doctor. His body moved with the quick, jerky motions of a mouse caught in a pantry. If this was the man who'd coldly murdered Lynnie...

"I've got to get to Elaina," she told Marcus. "I don't know how, but I've simply got to do it. Tonight."

"Be a neat trick," said Marcus. "The personal servant Barbara gave us is there for a reason. And it's not to be sure we don't run out of milk and cookies."

"I don't care," snapped Jessie. "I *am* going to see her. She knows something. I'm dead certain of that."

"You think she does. You can't be sure."

"I'm sure."

Marcus frowned curiously at her tone. "All right—what do you know that I don't?"

Jessie bit her lip. "I, uh—don't want to go into it right here."

"Here is just fine," he said firmly.

"Marcus—" Jessie sighed, leaned over, and whispered in his ear. "I know, dear, because Elaina Culbertson was outside my tent the night they let the horses loose. She warned me to get out."

"What!" Marcus's eyes went wide, and everyone at the table turned to stare. Marcus lowered his voice. "Why the hell didn't you tell me?"

"I was afraid you'd do something foolish."

"Like what?"

"I don't know. Strangle Lane Forsman?"

"I'm going to do that anyway," he said darkly. "Christ, Jessie—"

"Look, I'm *sorry*. I— Oh, hell, now what?"

Lane Forsman stood shakily at the head of the table. "Aw'right, folks. Got an annous—an an*nounce*-ment to make." He winked and gave a lopsided grin. "Inna morning, goin' to—goin' to have a—hell, what's going to be in the morning, huh?"

138

The guests laughed, and Barbara stood up and pushed back her chair. "What dear Lane is trying to say is that we are going to have a hunt in the morning. It's a very special kind of hunt, something I don't think you've experienced before." The guests shouted questions, but Barbara held up a hand. "Now that is all I'm going to say, all right? I don't want to spoil the surprise. All I'll tell you is—"

Barbara suddenly froze as the loud blast of a rifle sounded outside. Women shrieked, and men started to come to their feet.

"Hold it!" Lane shouted, and threw up his hands. He suddenly seemed to be cold sober. "Stay where you are—please. Our boys will handle it, whatever it is!"

The Forsmans' black-clad servants were already out of the room, running for the hall and the big front door. In a moment, a rattle of rifle and pistol fire echoed from the courtyard. Jessie looked at Marcus, who was perched intently on the edge of his chair.

For a moment there was nothing but silence. Then the shots started again. One of the black-suited hands ran into the room and drew Lane aside. Jessie glanced over her shoulder. Dr. Sacchetti was standing near the door, looking grim. *Now, what the hell is he doing out there?* she wondered.

Lane turned back to the table. His face was flushed, and the reassuring grin was clearly forced. "No problem," he said loudly. "It's all over. 'Fraid one of the ranch hands did a little too much celebrating and thought he was Billy the Kid. Passed out, thank heaven, 'fore anyone got hurt. Guess some people just can't hold their liquor." The guests laughed at him and Lane laughed with them.

The gunfire signaled the end of supper, and Jessie pulled Marcus quickly aside. "Talk to Amanda," she told him. "It'd be better if you did it than if I did. Tell her I've got to know where Elaina's room is." Marcus hesitated, and Jessie's green eyes shot him a warning. "Go on, Marcus—just do it!"

Marcus shrugged and wandered back to the table. He found Amanda, talked to her briefly, and started back for Jessie. Lane Forsman caught up and dogged his heels. "Wait now, I gotta talk to you two."

"About what?" Marcus said tightly.

Lane glanced over his shoulder. "I told the others we had a drunk out there. That's not true. Five or six men came over the wall. Got in the courtyard before the fellows at the gate could stop 'em. They were trying to get in *here*. At us. Four of my men are dead and a couple more hurt."

"Did you get any of them?" asked Jessie.

"Two. Both dead, damn it, or I'd sure find out who sent 'em. The others got away. Marcus, I know you don't much like me, and I can't help that. I'm sorry, 'cause I haven't done a damn thing to deserve bad feelings from you. Or you either, Jessie. I think we ought to work together on this. I said that before. Talk it over and see what we can come up with."

Marcus took a deep breath. "All right. If you like, Lane."

Forsman beamed. "You mean that?"

"I say what I mean. You ought to know that by now."

"Then we'll do it, by God, and I couldn't be more pleased. Right after the hunt tomorrow."

Jessie forced a smile. "Just what is this hunt all about? Barbara was kind of mysterious."

Lane gave her a sheepish grin. "It's a surprise. Hell, she'd have my head if I told you. Sleep well, now." Waving, he turned and stalked back to his guests.

"I take it you don't believe that nonsense any more than I do," said Jessie. She undid the buttons of her gown down to her waist, gathered up her skirts, and sat on the bed to take off her shoes.

"I believe in elves, fairies, and Lane Forsman," Marcus said solemnly. "In that order. Hell, how hard would it be to tell your boys to run out and fire off a bunch of rounds? No trouble at all."

"Yes, but why, Marcus? Why bother? Lane and Barbara know we're onto them. Why keep playing the game?"

Marcus gave her a long and thoughtful look. "Why do *we* keep pretending, Jessie? We came on this goddamn trip knowing the Forsmans are up to their necks in something. Where's the sense in that?"

Jessie took a breath and looked away. "It was a dumb thing to do, and I'm sorry. Does that make you happy?"

140

Marcus tossed his shirt aside, sat down beside her, and kissed her. "What's done is done, Jessie. All I care about now is getting us both out of here in one piece. I figure that's going to take a fair-sized effort."

Jessie turned and brushed strawberry hair over her bare shoulders. "You think so? Honestly, Marcus? I know that stampede was deliberate, but that was out on the trail. Would the Forsmans really try to kill us here? In their own house?"

"Hell, yes, they would," Marcus said grimly.

"I just can't see the cartel bringing that kind of attention to themselves. Whatever they're up to—and I still don't have the slightest idea what that is—it's important enough to protect. They'd like us both dead, but why foul their own nest? That doesn't make sense. Not when we— What are you *doing!*"

Marcus grinned. "Just, uh, trying to be of some help. That chemise is caught on your shoulders."

Jessie raised an eyebrow. "It's not *caught* there, friend. That's where it belongs."

"When you're dressed, sure. But when you're getting undressed . . ."

"Uh-huh. And who said I was?"

Marcus didn't answer. Instead, he slipped the light garment over her shoulders and down past the swell of her breasts. Cupping the firm mounds in his hands, he tilted them up gently and kissed first one nipple and then the other.

"Oh, Lord!" Jessie gasped. She held his head and drew it hard against her breasts, then suddenly sat up and pushed him away.

Marcus looked bewildered. "What's the matter?"

"Nothing is the matter," Jessie groaned, getting quickly to her feet and covering her breasts. "Except I've got something to do, and if you start that, I sure as hell won't do it."

Marcus's face fell. "You're talking about Elaina." He shook his head adamantly. "I don't like it, Jessie. It's a bad idea."

"I know it is. What else is new?" She turned, saw the expression in his eyes, and ran into his arms. "Oh, damn, Marcus—I'm scared to death and you know it. Don't try to talk me out of it. Please. Because it wouldn't be hard at all . . ."

* * *

When Marcus called him in, Aurochs frowned, his great shoulders filling the frame of the door. He sniffed the air and scanned the room with his eyes.

"What you wanting?" he growled. "Need somethin' from kitchen?"

"No, just a little help," Marcus replied. He pointed at the washstand in the corner. "I'd like that moved over there."

Aurochs blinked his small eyes. "Why?"

"Because I like it over there," Marcus said firmly.

"Hunh!" Aurochs grunted. "Belongs here. Not there."

Marcus flushed and pulled himself up to his full height. "Damn it, are you in the habit of questioning Senator Forsman's guests?" He was a big man, but his head barely reached Aurochs' chin. "I can wake him and get permission if you want!"

Aurochs gritted his teeth, and picked up the table with one hand.

Jessie waited behind the door that separated her room from Marcus's until she heard Aurochs enter. Then she moved quickly to the door to the hall, opened it quietly, peered outside, and slipped into the corridor. She was grateful for the darkness; only a dim kerosene lamp hung at one end of the hall. Pausing at the corner past a heavy Spanish table, she checked the corridor ahead. As she'd guessed, one of the black-clad guards was making his rounds. Lane and Barbara were taking no chances on guests wandering about.

When the man disappeared, she slipped into the hall, praying that Amanda was right. Second door, then the third. She tapped as loudly as she dared, one eye on the darkness to her left. Someone moved inside and the door opened a crack. "Mrs. Culbertson," Jessie whispered, "let me in, please. I must talk to you!"

Elaina hesitated, then moved quickly aside. Jessie closed the door softly behind her. The older woman was wrapped in a robe. She stared at Jessie with wide, frightened eyes. "What are you doing here? If they find you—"

"It's all right," Jessie assured her. "They won't. I promise. I wouldn't put you in any danger."

"That is something you cannot promise, young lady," Elaina said shortly. Grasping the head of her cane, she lowered herself

142

to a chair. "You don't know what you're doing. You should never have come to this place. Never! My God, Miss Starbuck, whatever possessed you to put yourself in their hands!"

"I had to," Jessie said flatly. "There was no other way to learn what they're doing. And thank you, Mrs. Culbertson. You saved my life, and I'm grateful."

Elaina's eyes softened for just a moment. "You are in grave danger, Jessica. They can't afford to let you stay alive. Not now. You know too much about them. Far too much."

Jessie leaned forward. "But I don't—that's just it. I know they're hiding some terrible scheme, but I don't know what it is. Do you? Have you any idea?"

Elaina's eyes brightened. "Oh, yes. I know exactly what they're doing. They don't even try to keep it from me anymore. They know it frightens me. The more I know, the more I—" Her voice broke and she looked straight at Jessie. "They take young women, Jessica, beautiful young women, and train them in the arts of seduction, the ways to use men and keep them under control. They place these women in positions of power, as the wives and mistresses of men who run the nation's business, the government—"

"My God!" Jessie stared in disbelief. Suddenly all the loose ends seemed to fall into place. "Of course, it had to be something like that. And Barbara Forsman—"

"Barbara was one of them. The worst of them all, I think. She is a cruel woman without a conscience—a woman who would do anything to get her way. Anything."

"She has some kind of power over you, doesn't she?" Jessie asked softly. "You're frightened of her, I saw that from the beginning."

Elaina looked appalled. "Frightened of her? My God, Jessica, she has ruined my life, taken everything I had, everything I held dear. Do you know how I feel, talking to you like this? You are a greater threat to me than Barbara. If she ever learns what I have done . . ."

"Then why are you confiding in me?"

Elaina's hands shook. "Because I—cannot live with myself anymore. I cannot let this thing happen any longer!"

Slowly the whole story came out. Elaina told Jessie how Barbara had gained her trust, becoming almost like a daughter to a woman who had none of her own. Elaina's husband was dead, and she was flattered and grateful that a lovely young woman would show her so much kindness and attention. Barbara's friends became Elaina's friends as well, and were invited to Elaina's fine parties. Some of the young men Barbara knew advised Elaina how best to run the Culbertson financial interests. The men her late husband had trusted were slowly forced out of the picture. Too late, Elaina realized what Barbara really was—and that control of the Culbertson fortune was out of her hands.

"Who were these people?" asked Jessie. "Do you know? Do you know where they came from?"

Elaina sighed. "I only know they are terrible, powerful men who control a great business empire all over the world."

"Europeans? Prussians?" asked Jessie.

"Why, yes." Elaina looked surprised. "How did you know that?"

Jessie didn't answer. "It's Barbara, isn't it? Barbara's the one who controls the operation. Lane doesn't have much to do with it, does he?"

Elaina's face twisted in anger and disgust. "Lane Forsman is a fool! Always has been. Known the family for years. Barbara used my social position and money to meet him. *He* didn't need any persuading, I'll tell you that. Knows all about the operation and does whatever Barbara and her masters tell him. God, I despise the man!"

Jessie didn't want to ask, didn't really want to know, but it was something she had to do. "Lynnie was one of them, then. One of the women like Barbara."

Elaina nodded, then reached out and touched Jessie's hand. "She was trained right here, Jessica. Where Barbara keeps the girls until they're ready. Barbara recruited her on one of her trips to Europe. She seemed like such a nice girl, really."

"You don't have to say that," Jessie sighed. "They couldn't force a woman to do what Barbara and the others do. You'd have to want to, wouldn't you? I kept thinking of her as the Lynnie I knew long ago, and that was a mistake. They were grooming her for Marcus, weren't they? Then something happened. Do you—do you know what it was? Why did they have to kill her?"

144

"I don't know, my dear. They don't need much of a reason. She was a threat to them in some way, that's all I can say." She smiled and patted Jessie's hand. "Perhaps your friend was still something of what you imagined her to be."

A thought suddenly struck Jessie. "There was a girl, a young girl at your place, the day of the shooting—"

Elaina's face went white. "You saw her? If they'd known that. . . . Yes, she's one of Lane's playthings. A girl from here. Barbara pretends to be jealous of Lane's needs, but I assure you she doesn't care. The drink and the women keep him in line. He does what they tell him to do, and that's all that matters."

"That shooting, the incident in the courtyard tonight—"

Elaina shook her head. "I don't know what happened tonight. It frightened me terribly. They're worried about something, I know that." She remembered something and looked at Jessie. "Lane's wound—it's fakery, of course. He wasn't hit at all. The whole incident was staged, with one real killing—the young marshal who was protecting you. When they learned you didn't intend to quit at all, they decided to be victims themselves." A quick sparkle of amusement touched her eyes. "I knew you weren't fooled, my dear. You are far too intelligent a young woman for that."

Jessie groaned and looked at the ceiling. "If I'm so all-fired smart, how come I didn't figure all this out before I got in a spot like this?" She stood then, and squeezed the older woman's hand. "We're going to get out of this somehow, Mrs. Culbertson. All of us. I don't know how, but we will."

Elaina stared at her with no expression at all. "I don't think I'm even scared anymore, do you know? They've taken everything from me but my life. Now that doesn't mean much, either."

"Don't say that," Jessie pleaded. "I told you we're going to get out of this." She turned then, and listened at the door.

"Jessica, wait—"

Jessie turned, and Elaina held out a trembling hand. "Don't try anything foolish. Please. I think you and Marcus are safe as long as you're here. I don't *know* that, but I don't think they'll dare try anything more—until you and the others start home."

"I'd suspected that."

Elaina strained forward in her chair. "But after you leave here, Jessica, they will murder you any way they can!"

★

Chapter 16

When he awoke, he smelled the acrid odor of his own sweat. Opening his eyes, he blinked up at the darkness and took a deep breath. His body felt different, not the same at all, and in a moment he understood why. He was cold, but it was not the same chill he'd felt before. He'd passed out when they carried him back to the cell, but sometime in the night his fever had broken.

Ki breathed a long sigh of relief. He was weak, but at least his mind was clear. Turning over slowly, he raised himself up on his knees. He felt lightheaded, but he willed himself not to fall. He forced his thoughts from his thirst, the gnawing ache in his belly. The important thing now was to make his body work, get his arms and legs functioning again. If he let himself go weak, he was finished . . .

The thought brought a hollow laugh to his lips. *Where the hell do you think you are now? They've got you and it's over . . .*

He shook the thought aside, put one hand in front of the other, brought his left knee up, and then his right. *Got to get*

147

to Annie . . . find Jessie . . . get out of this place . . .

When his head bumped the end of the cell, he laughed aloud and collapsed, and let the darkness pull him under again . . .

Something was wrong . . .

The ground was moving swiftly by beneath him, bobbing up and down in a crazy pattern. He closed his eyes, opened them, and looked at it again. Bile rose to his throat. He let the sticky fluid trail from his mouth.

Draped over a horse . . . going downhill . . . gray, foggy light meant it was morning. Where the hell were they taking him now?

In a moment the rocky path beneath him turned to a lush blanket of grass. Somewhere in the back of his mind he knew they'd left the high retreat and moved into the hills. He could smell the fresh dew, the cool scents of dawn . . .

The horse stopped. Someone squatted and cut a rope. Ki fell in a heap and the man laughed. They picked him up by his heels, dragged him a few yards, and dropped him again. He could see them now. They were dressed in black, but none of them was Aurochs. *Be thankful for small favors . . .*

The men picked him up and dropped him on something hard. Wood. Wood and the smell of new paint. They spread-eagled him and tied him down, put a gag in his mouth, and went away.

When he was certain they were gone, he tried his ropes to see if they'd left any play. Turning his head, he could see the edge of the board. It extended past his arms and legs a good two feet. The board was flat, cut in some irregular shape. Why? What was it for? Looking past the board, all he could see was grass—high grass all around, a good two or three feet high.

He arched his back as best he could, then let himself fall back. The board swayed, which meant there was a hole underneath. He banged his head against the wood. A hollow sound came back. He took a deep breath and lay still, trying to picture himself standing just beyond his own body. What did he look like from there? A man tied to a board over a hole in the ground. It didn't make a damned bit of sense. He lay back and looked at the brightening sky. The sun felt good on his body.

148

He tried to stay awake, but exhaustion took him under once more...

Smoke-blue clouds hung on ragged peaks to the east. The sun blazed over the high tips of the Rockies, turning the landscape below a brilliant gold. Jessie sniffed cool air and guided her mount down the stony path.

"I've got to be crazy," she told Marcus. "I feel great this morning. Somehow that doesn't seem right."

Marcus shot her a lazy grin. "I don't know, I thought you felt great last night. At least everything *I* could feel was—"

Jessie brushed hair out of her eyes. "That's not what I meant, and you know it. Marcus, one way or another we are getting *out* of this place today," she said soberly. "I know all I want to know. Billy Vail or the U.S. Cavalry or whoever else we can holler up can finish the job. Mrs. Culbertson figures we're safe on Barbara's home ground, but I don't."

"I couldn't agree more," said Marcus. He nodded over his shoulder at the scowling hulk of Aurochs, riding behind them. "How about him. You think he'll mind?"

"Don't be funny." snapped Jessie. She slapped the butt of the Winchester by her saddle. "Giving us rifles was a mistake. She's too damn sure of herself."

"Maybe she's got good reason."

Jessie didn't answer. The sheer stone walls of the granite mesa were now directly overhead, hiding the Forsmans' retreat perched on the top. Below, the first horses in the column had already reached the bottom. Lane was there, looking half-sober for a change, and Barbara, chatting gaily with her guests. Jessie was surprised to see Elaina sitting her horse. When she'd left the poor woman the night before, she'd looked as if she'd take to her bed for the day. Most likely, Jessie decided, she didn't have a choice...

Barbara waited until they were all gathered around her in a thick grove of Ponderosa pine. Jessie noted darkly that she was as fresh and breathtaking as ever.

"I told you all last night that this was going to be a surprise," she said brightly. "A *different* kind of hunt. You'll be using real rifles and ammunition, but you won't be shooting at real

149

game." She waited, letting her words sink in, enjoying the puzzled chatter of the others. "We'll be shooting at targets," she explained. "But not just any old targets. They'll pop up off the ground when you least expect them—deer and bear and antelope and everything." She bit her lip and gave the nearest male a mischievous wink. "You men are going to have to be on your toes today, because the ladies get an equal chance to shoot. I know some of these women, and you just might get beaten!"

The men roared, and the women joined in with shrill volleys of laughter. Jessie and Marcus exchanged a look.

Barbara turned her mount in an elegant circle and smiled at her husband. "Lane's got a prize for the highest-scoring couple. A case of the very finest Moët champagne!"

The guests cheered. Marcus nodded to Jessie to pull her mount aside, out of earshot of their black-suited guardian.

"I don't like it. What the hell do you think she's up to?"

Before Jessie could answer, Barbara called out and motioned them over. "Jessie, Marcus—come on, we're getting started!"

Jessie felt a quick moment of cold, unreasoning fear. Something she couldn't name reached out and touched her, and it was all she could do to keep from kicking her mount into a run and fleeing that place without looking back.

"Jessie, easy . . ." Marcus's strong hand gripped her arm.

"Yeah, thanks." Jessie let out a breath. "I'm fine, Marcus." She glanced over her shoulder and looked quickly away. Aurochs sat his mount right behind her, his bulk nearly dwarfing the big stallion he rode.

Barbara and Lane led the party due west, away from the high retreat. Tree-covered hills bounded the lush green valley on either side. Jessie decided they were a few miles northeast of the trail they'd taken from the south, past the low foothills that held the Forsmans' great herds of cattle. Glancing to the left and right, she could see the black-clad outriders ranging through the grass, flanking the small column of guests. It was easy to spot Aurochs—he was bigger than any two others of the Forsmans' hands.

"At least the bastard's not breathing down my back," said Jessie. "Lord, that man gives me the creeps."

One of the men just ahead came to a halt, and Barbara reined in her mount. "We're in the target area now," she called back to the others. "Elaina, dear, I'd be most honored if you'd take the first shot."

Elaina Culbertson turned white. "I haven't shot in a long time," she muttered, showing Barbara a sickly smile. "I'd really rather not."

"Nonsense. You'll do just fine."

"Barbara—"

"Oh, I insist, Elaina."

Elaina bit her lip, pulled her Winchester out of its saddle scabbard, and levered a shell into the chamber. Barbara looked pleased. "Everybody watch now. I know Elaina's going to do well."

The outriders moved forward, staying well behind Barbara and Mrs. Culbertson. Lane looked over his shoulder, caught Jessie's eye, and gave her a foolish grin. Jessie pretended she didn't see.

Suddenly a target sprang up off the ground some fifty yards ahead. It was painted to look like an elk with a full head of antlers. Elaina raised the rifle to her shoulder and squeezed off four quick shots. The guests cheered, and Barbara held up her hand to quiet them.

"Wait now," she called out. "Let's not applaud till we see how Mrs. Culbertson did!"

A rider dismounted and ran to the target. In a moment he'd pasted three white circles the size of Morgan dollars on the cut-out elk. When he stepped aside, everyone yelled and clapped loudly. The shots were well-grouped along the animal's painted shoulder.

Barbara gaped at Elaina, then forced a quick smile. "See, I told you you could do it. Come on now, everyone. It's going to be hard to beat that!"

Jessie caught a glimpse of Elaina's face. She looked as if she could easily raise the rifle and plant the rest of her shots in Barbara's back.

Marcus looked at Jessie. "If I were Barbara, I wouldn't let that old lady get behind me. She isn't a bad shot."

"No, she isn't. Barbara wasn't expecting that, either. Serves the bitch right."

The fat cattleman and his skinny wife were next. A few moments later, a target shaped like a bear rearing up on its hind legs popped into view. The couple fired a volley of shots, firing until their rifles were empty. Jessie saw the rounds clip grass and raise dirt, and knew that neither of the two had hit a thing. When a rider pasted four white circles in the bear's ample belly, she was certain the men had been told to make sure the guests weren't embarrassed.

Jessie understood now just how the targets worked. When the shooting party approached, one of the black-clad riders stationed himself next to the column, slid off his horse, and waited. Ropes of some sort were hidden in the grass, stretching fifty or so yards from the target to the "puller." The targets were under tension, and when the rider yanked the rope, the "game" sprang into view.

"Hell of a lot of trouble for next to nothing, if you ask me," Jessie grumbled. "Any kid over ten could hit something like that."

"These folks aren't exactly kids," Marcus reminded her.

Ki opened his eyes, then shut them once more against the sun. For a good quarter of an hour he'd heard shots. One quick volley, then nothing. A few minutes later came another, this time closer than the first. The third grouping was quite close, less than half a mile away.

A hot breeze rustled the grass, bringing the sound of voices. Ki strained against his bonds, raised his head from the board, and listened. A woman laughed. A man spoke in a loud, booming voice, but his words were lost on the wind.

People were moving toward him, firing rifles. Ki gnawed at his gag and tried to shake the stinging sweat from his eyes. What the hell were they doing? Who were they?

He had no illusions that anyone was coming to help. He had no friends in this place, only men who wanted to hurt him.

A vivid picture of Annie appeared in his mind. She was frightened, her face frozen in terror. A low moan of anger and frustration was lost behind his gag. He'd tried. But trying wasn't enough. He'd failed her, and failed Jessie as well . . .

Ki strained against his bonds as a new sound reached his ears. It was as if a heavy door had suddenly slammed into place. Shouts followed the sound, and this time he could hear bullets whining above the grass overhead. Damn—whatever it was, it was getting close!

His heartbeat quickened in sudden, unreasoning fear. The shots. The sound like a door. Not a door—something else. He tried to put a name to it and couldn't. A terrible panic was growing within him. He tried to shake it off, but it wouldn't let go.

The tiger was loose again. He could feel it, smell its hot breath on the wind . . .

Desperately he wrenched his arms and legs trying to tear the ropes free. The cords cut into his flesh and brought blood, but Ki felt nothing at all.

They've staked me out to kill me. This is where I am going to die . . .

He faced the thought calmly and knew it was so. He firmly believed a samurai could sense such things, that he could feel death coming. *The smell of the beast was dank and heavy on the air. It was near. He could almost see its face . . .*

Amanda and Charlie van Rijn brought their weapons to bear, and fired. When the rider counted holes, Jessie knew he'd found no need to make the couple look good. She'd seen the chips of wood fly from the target. Amanda clapped like a child when she saw the results. Out of ten shots between the two rifles, eight had peppered the pronghorn antelope's chest.

Barbara's golden hair blew like silk over her shoulders. She turned and danced her horse up to Jessie. "You and Marcus are next. You're going to have to go some to beat Amanda and Charlie." She paused and looked Jessie straight in the eye. "I understand you're a pretty fair shot."

"I've been known to hit what I shoot at," Jessie said flatly. She saw Lane look right at her. Dr. Sacchetti sat motionless beside Mrs. Culbertson, bright sun dancing off his glasses.

Barbara turned around in the saddle to face the others. "I've got a marvelous idea," she said. "Why don't we let Jessie take the target herself, and see if she can beat Marcus's score on the next one? We'll find out who's best here, the ladies or the men!"

The others cheered Barbara on. Jessie exchanged a curious

look with Marcus, but he was glaring at the ground.

"I've got a better idea," said Jessie. "I'll take this target, Barbara, and *you* take the next."

Barbara studied her for a moment. "Fine," she said softly. "I accept the challenge, Jessie." There was a quick gleam of triumph in her cold blue eyes. "And how about a little side bet?" she suggested. "A hundred dollars for every shot in the heart?"

Jessie grinned. "To hell with that," she snapped. "Let's make it a thousand!"

Barbara wet her lips. "Whatever you want, dear." She danced her mount aside to let Jessie take the lead...

★

Chapter 17

Jessie swept her eyes over the thick sea of grass. She held the rifle loosely against her breast, letting her body move with the mount's easy gait. Barbara rode ahead and to the right. Marcus was just behind her. She couldn't see his face, but she could feel his disapproval.

He's right, damn it. What am I doing playing games with Barbara Forsman? The woman wants me dead, and I'm betting on some fool target!

A sound reached her ears, a deep and throaty growl. She twisted in the saddle and faced Aurochs' scowling features. The look in his eyes sent a chill up her spine. *That's all I need,* she thought grimly, *Barbara's pet bear crawling up my back...*

Out of the corner of her eye she saw the black-clad rider slip easily off his horse, and knew he was there to pull the target. Once more she heard Aurochs' angry rumbling. *You son of a bitch,* she thought, *if you think you're going to throw me off with that...*

Suddenly the target sprang out of the grass. A big, shaggy-humped buffalo was painted on the board. In one motion, Jessie swept the Winchester up to her shoulder, let out a breath, and let the barrel drop neatly on the target.

Aurochs roared—a sound like all the pain and anger in the world. His horse slammed hard into Jessie's, nearly jolting her out of the saddle. Jessie pulled the trigger and the shot went wild. A massive fist spun the rifle out of her grasp. The giant bolted past her like a storm, his flat features twisted out of shape.

"*Aurochs!*" Barbara shouted, but Aurochs didn't hear. Suddenly, Sacchetti came out of nowhere, black coat flying behind his spindly frame. He rode straight at Aurochs, shaking his fist in anger. His horse slammed into the big man's mount, spilling them both from the saddle. Aurochs sprang to his feet, took one step toward Sacchetti, and jerked him off the ground by his hair. Sacchetti shrieked, his legs churning the air.

"He—is—*mine!*" Aurochs bellowed. "*I* kill 'im—you promise!"

Sacchetti wailed in horror. Aurochs' hand snaked under his shirt, and something bright whirred in the sun. Sacchetti's body vanished in the grass. Blood spilled from the severed head in Aurochs' hand. He looked at it, tossed it away, and ran for the target.

A woman screamed. Jessie went rigid as she stared at the terrible figure. *It's him! Oh, God, no, it's him!*

"Jessie—look out!"

Marcus's shout brought her around. Barbara's face was a mask of anger—she stuck the Colt out straight in trembling hands, pointing the barrel at Jessie's face. Marcus kicked his mount and bolted between them. The pistol roared. Marcus cried out, wobbled in the saddle, and brought the butt of his rifle up hard. Barbara grunted and flew off the back of her horse. Spitting blood, she crawled under the frightened mounts after the Colt. Jessie slid off her horse, grabbed the pistol, and kicked Barbara away.

"Come on," Marcus shouted. "Up here, Jessie!"

Jessie turned, grabbed the back of his saddle, and pulled herself up fast. Marcus spurred the mount savagely, nearly throwing Jessie off.

"Christ, Marcus, are you all right?"

"She's a lousy shot," he said tightly. "I think you would've won that bet."

Jessie risked a look over her shoulder. Three loose horses were hightailing it south through the grass. Several of the guests sat stunned on their mounts. The banker shook his fist, trying to stop his frightened mare. A skinny woman in black ran shrieking in a circle.

"Marcus!" yelled Jessie. "Over there!"

Three of Barbara's gunmen were riding toward them fast. Marcus cursed and pulled his horse around as rifles opened up across the grass. Jessie's buffalo target was to the left, forty yards southward. She'd forgotten about Aurochs. He suddenly stepped from behind the target, stared at her, and turned on his heel.

"Marcus!" Jessie's hands dug into his back. "Marcus, that madman's got someone. He's carrying someone off!"

"What? He can't be!"

Aurochs turned and looked back, and they both saw him heft the limp body over his shoulder.

"Oh, Christ!" Jessie's eyes went wide with disbelief. "It's Ki! Marcus, it's Ki!" The landscape swam about her.

"Hold on, damn it!" Marcus shouted as he rode straight at Aurochs. The killer stared, terrible pain and anger twisting his features. He stopped, took a few steps backward, and threw Ki from him. Then he turned and ran, zigzagging to avoid the shots that Marcus pumped in his direction. Jessie threw herself from Marcus's horse as he reined in, and ran for Ki. Marcus fired a shot for good measure at Aurochs, then dismounted himself and took a bead on one of the pursuing riders. The first shot missed, but the second lifted a gunman from the saddle. The others drew rein fast, leaped to the ground, and began firing at Marcus, Jessie, and Ki from prone positions in the tall grass. Marcus's spooked horse took off at a gallop.

Bullets snapped through the air around them, and Marcus took one of Ki's arms and Jessie grabbed the other, and together they dragged him into the cover of a large boulder. A couple of shots whined off the rock, then the firing stopped as the gunmen realized that their quarry was inaccessible.

Jessie held Ki in her arms, tears wetting her cheeks. Ki's features were slack, and there was a dark and ugly bruise on his forehead. Ki opened his eyes and smiled weakly.

"Jessie," he said, "you do show up at the damnedest times . . ."

Jessie laughed and helped him sit with his back against the boulder. "Oh, Ki," she said, "You are a sight for sore eyes, but you look awful! What on earth have those bastards done to you?"

Ki just shook his head.

"What are you doing out here?" Jessie asked.

"They tied me to the back of that target," Ki replied. "The idea was to let you kill me."

Jessie's expression was grim as she said, "It figures. The cartel does come up with some original solutions to its problems. But why did Aurochs spoil my aim? He gave away their whole scheme."

"He's dangerous, but not very smart where his pride is concerned," Ki said. "He got it in his head that he had to be the one to kill me. Jealousy takes strange forms. I'm just glad he decided not to kill me on the spot. I thought I was dead when he came up with that bloody hatchet, but he just smacked me across the head and cut me down. Probably figured on taking me someplace where he could do the job *very* slowly . . ."

"I hate to break up the reunion," Marcus said as he took cartridges from his jacket pocket and loaded them into his Winchester's magazine, "but we've only got two guns between us—not counting Jessie's derringer, which wouldn't be any use at this range anyway—and my horse is gone. Our ammunition won't hold out forever, so the question is, what do we do now? I'm sure those hardcases out there are going to start spreading out to see if they can surround us, so we'd better figure out how we're going to get out of here."

"If this tall grass can provide cover for them, it can do the same for us," Ki observed. "We just have to keep low."

"Guess it's the only way," Marcus replied. "Maybe I can carry Ki if we can get him up on my back—"

"No need," Ki said. "I think I can manage."

Several bullets whined off the boulder, and Marcus said, "Sounds like they're getting closer. If we're going to make our move, I reckon now's the time."

Jessie nodded. "Right. Let's do it!"

She could see the side of the hill and the tops of the trees over the grass, fifty, sixty yards away. It might as well be a hundred miles, she thought darkly. Ki touched her shoulder and pushed her down. Jessie heard the squeak of a saddle, and hooves pounding the ground to her right. The rider called out. Another man answered. The rider pulled his mount around and galloped off.

Marcus nodded silently over his shoulder, came to a crouch, and moved forward. Jessie and Ki followed. She tried not to think about Aurochs; he was out here somewhere, too. The grotesque image of Sacchetti's bloody head came to her.

Marcus motioned them to a stop. "We'll have to run for it from here," he told them. "There's ten, maybe fifteen yards of clearing and then we're into the trees."

"They know that too," whispered Jessie.

"Sure they do. Any suggestions?"

"It's a lot of grass," said Ki. "They know we're coming out, but they don't know where."

Jessie forced a grin. "What are we waiting for? I'm getting real tired of crawling." She checked Barbara's Colt, and glanced at the two men. At Marcus's nod, they burst out of the grass into the open, sprinting for the cover of the trees. As they ran, she saw four black-garbed riders coming out of the grass to her left. She shouted at Marcus. He turned, fired two quick shots, and ran. Jessie dove for cover and heard Ki land behind her. Marcus was already on his knees, bracing the Winchester on the trunk of a tree. He squeezed off two careful shots, and threw back his head and laughed as the riders turned their mounts around fast, kicking up dust.

"That'll hold 'em a minute. Let's get a little higher before they come at us again."

"Up there," said Ki. He pointed through the pines to a high stone outcrop. They made their way up the hill into the thick tumble of lichen-covered boulders. Ki quickly surveyed their perch, then dropped beside Jessie. "It's a good spot. They'll have to come after us on foot, without cover," He looked at Marcus and frowned. "We'd better take a look at that wound. You're losing a little blood."

Marcus waved him off. "Forget it. She damn near missed."

Ki ignored him and loosened Marcus's shirt to bare the wound. The bullet had creased the fleshy part of his waist and left a neat red furrow. Jessie tore a strip from Marcus's shirt and cleaned it as best she could.

Marcus flinched at her touch, and grinned. "Told you she was a lousy shot, Jessie."

"She wasn't aiming at you," Jessie reminded him. "She was trying to kill me."

"Who?" Ki looked puzzled. "Who are we talking about?"

"Barbara. Barbara Forsman." She touched Ki's arm and sighed. "You and I have a lot of catching up to do, you know? I'm still trying to figure what you're doing alive." She glanced up at Marcus. "Any sign yet?"

Marcus shook his head. "They'll be here. Probably waiting for help." He reached in his pocket and counted shells with his fingers. "I've got about three spare rounds, Jessie. And twelve in the rifle. How about you?"

"Three. I already checked."

Marcus muttered to himself and stared through the trees at the valley. "It's going to cost the bastards. We've got the high ground."

He didn't need to say more; she knew exactly what he was thinking. They could make a good showing, but in the end there was no place to go. Eventually it would end right here.

A thought suddenly struck her, and she sat up straight. No, that wasn't quite true. There were Amanda and Charlie van Rijn, as well as the other two couples and Elaina. Jessie's blood ran cold. Barbara couldn't let them go, not after what they'd seen. Whatever she'd had in mind for the two of them, this wasn't it. Staking Ki out to get killed was just a little extra madness—not part of the plan at all. Aurochs had turned everything upside down. Now Barbara would have to do away with seven of Denver's most prominent citizens—and Elaina's riders as well. Jessie wondered just how the hell she intended to handle that.

"What happened to Lane?" she asked Marcus abruptly. "Everything happened so fast, I didn't even see him."

"I did," Marcus said wryly. "He left Barbara and took off like a scared rabbit."

"Figures." She turned to Ki and gave him a warm smile. "For a man who got blown in a million pieces, you don't look half bad." She touched his brow lightly. "You doing all right, old friend?"

160

"I've been better—and worse," he said stoically.

"They had you up there in the retreat?"

Ki nodded. "I got out once and found Annie. That must have been last night. I'm not sure."

Jessie's mouth fell open. "Annie? Lord, is she alive too?"

Ki looked puzzled, then understood. "I'm sorry. You couldn't know. She was alive when they took us. I don't know what they may have done with her by now."

"Oh, Ki—"

"Hold it," Marcus said sharply, "we've got company."

Jessie and Ki moved up for a look. Two men sat on their horses in the high grass, well out of range. The others left their mounts and quickly crossed the clearing for the cover of the trees. Jessie counted seven black-shirted gunmen.

"There will be more," Ki said softly. "They will work their way up the slope to get behind us, while the men below keep us busy."

Marcus kept low, letting the men come, watching them work their way up the hill from tree to tree. Ki crouched beside him while Jessie moved carefully around the rear of their perch. She studied the hillside above, watching for shadows that didn't belong among the straight-trunked pines. They couldn't afford surprise intruders now—not with only a rifle and a pistol between them.

Suddenly the hill echoed with thunder as gunmen sent a withering volley into the rocks. Shards of rock went flying; pine needles fluttered to earth. Marcus didn't move. The deafening gunfire stopped. Marcus looked at Ki and grinned. Seconds later, the rifles started again. Marcus counted silently to himself, then snaked his weapon quickly over the edge of the boulder. Four gunmen were climbing the slope in the open, pumping lead up the hill. Marcus shot the first one in the face, then swept his rifle to the right and fired again. His target dropped his gun and grabbed his belly. Marcus ducked back to cover. Angry shouts came from below, and a hail of lead peppered the rocks.

"They won't try that again soon," snapped Marcus.

"No. But they'll try something else," said Ki. He glanced over his shoulder and caught Jessie's eye. "Anything moving?" Jessie shook her head. "Keep your eyes open," he told her. "There will be."

161

"I'm trying to figure how many are out there," said Marcus. "Those so-called servants that Barbara dresses up in black are obviously the toughs she can count on."

"Like Aurochs."

"Uh-huh. The ranch hands wouldn't be in this at all. More than likely they don't know anything about it."

Ki studied the branches overhead. "I'd guess there are a dozen or more in Aurochs' crew. There were nearly that many after me last night."

Marcus didn't seem surprised. "That was you, then."

"And Annie." Ki balled his fists in anger. "I had her. I had her out of there, damn it."

"I wouldn't blame myself for—"

"Ki! Marcus!" Jessie pointed frantically up the hill. Marcus held his position, and Ki crawled quickly up to meet her.

"Over there. To the right." Jessie pointed past a steep ridge of granite slanting up the hill through the trees. Ki watched for a moment. A dark figure moved. Then another and another.

Ki cursed under his breath. "They're doing it right. Trying to get above us."

"If we move over a little to the left, we can still stay under cover."

"No." Ki shook his head firmly. "That's what they want, Jessie. Flush us out and force us over there. When we get there, they'll be waiting for us." He craned his neck to look up the hill. "We've got to go up there, where they are. Only we've got to beat them to it."

Jessie looked appalled. "God, that's practically straight up!"

Marcus edged his way to them. "I'm afraid you're right," he said grimly. "It's about the only chance we've got. Ki, if you—"

A shot whined wildly through the trees. Lead splintered stone at Ki's shoulder. He grabbed Jessie and rolled her roughly to cover. Marcus turned on his back, pulled off two quick shots, and scampered to safety. A rain of bullets snapped at his heels.

"Damn!" Marcus hunched down beside Jessie and Ki. "Didn't take 'em long, did it?"

"Start climbing," said Ki. "We can't stay here another second. Marcus, you take the lead. Jessie, get between us and

162

give me your pistol." She did as he asked, and Ki tucked Barbara's gun into the waist of his trousers. Normally, Ki disdained the use of firearms, but with God knew how many armed men in pursuit, and two other people to protect, he wasn't about to engage in philosophical quibbles.

As they climbed, rifle fire sounded from above, and was joined by a fresh volley from below. Ki climbed faster, knowing the gunmen had reached the perch they'd just abandoned.

Suddenly the sheltered chimney they'd followed came to an end. Marcus took Jessie's hand and they began working their way laboriously around a sheer wall of granite, searching for another way up. Ki braced himself and watched them. Shots rained down from above, but they still had cover.

He heard the sound then, and froze. They were scrambling up the rock just behind him, making no effort to hide their movements. Ki looked over his shoulder. Jessie was gone. Marcus clung to the wall; he turned, saw that Ki wasn't moving, and frantically motioned him forward. Ki held up a palm and waved him on, then turned and flattened himself against stone as best he could. Taking a deep breath, he drew the Colt and waited. The gunman was breathing hard. Boots ground against rock, and a hand appeared only inches from Ki's shoulder. He held himself back another second, then launched himself from the boulder, slammed his left foot hard against the far wall, and kicked out with his right. The man gasped and fell back, taking the gunman behind him down with him.

Ki grinned and leaned back in his crevice. A cry of pain and a scattering of angry curses came from below. Someone fired a few shots in his direction for the hell of it.

Ki didn't move. In a moment he heard the scraping of boots on stone. Without looking, he knew what they were doing. One man was climbing. Another waited below, covering his companion with a rifle. They knew where he was; if he poked his head out an inch, they'd blow it off.

A scattering of shots came from above. Ki prayed that Jessie was all right.

The man was getting close. Ki had to hand it to him, the fellow had guts. He pulled the gun from his waistband and waited. The man stopped. Ki pulled himself up the crevice as high as he could, pressing his back and the soles of his feet

163

against the rock, drawing himself off the ground. He listened. For a moment there was nothing. Then, so fast he almost caught Ki off guard, the gunman threw himself into the open, coming in low, as Ki had predicted. Both pistols fired at once. Ki saw the astonishment in the man's eyes as he slid out of sight— then miraculously seemed to come at Ki again. Now it was Ki's turn to be surprised; they'd sent up two men at once, one right behind the other. Ki squeezed the trigger and knew he'd missed, fired again, and saw the bullet hit home. The man didn't stop—he was enormous, almost as big as Aurochs. Ki fired again and the Colt clicked empty. The man grabbed Ki's throat in a grip of iron and slammed him hard against stone. Ki brought up a hand between the man's arms and smashed upward against the cartilage of the killer's nose with the heel of his hand. The man lost his footing, but retained his grip, and Ki knew they were going down the hill together...

"Marcus!" Jessie went rigid, her green eyes dark with fright. "That was Ki—he's still down there!"

Marcus gripped her arm. "Jessie, we can't go back."

"Well, I'm not going to leave him!"

"Damn it, he—" Gunfire cut off his words. Marcus held her to him as lead whined around them.

Jessie searched the terrain; there was no place to go. They were cut off above and behind. The slope to the left dropped off into nothing. The rocks ahead offered cover, a few more minutes of safety. But after that— Would Barbara try to take them alive? The answer came quickly. What the hell for?

"Come on," Marcus said sharply. "We can't stay here!" He held out his hand and Jessie took it. Together they crouched and ran for the circle of boulders. A rifle opened up to their right. Bullets stitched a path across their way, and Marcus pulled Jessie aside. He tried to run back the way they'd come, but the sniper forced them forward, close to the edge of the slope. Marcus turned and emptied his rifle. Jessie backed cautiously down the hill, trying desperately to stay on her feet. Marcus threw himself to cover beside her, sending a shower of stones down the slope. Jessie reached out to catch him, and held him for an instant before his hand slipped away.

Marcus! Jessie shouted as a river of dirt and stone gave

164

way beneath her boots. She reached out frantically to stop her fall. Something hard hit her thigh, and a jolt of raw pain tore at her side. She slammed to a stop at the bottom, her foot in Marcus's chest. Marcus grunted and tried to sit up. Jessie crawled to him and touched his cheek.

"Are you all right? My God, you're as white as a ghost!"

"Damn it, Jessie, I think I broke something. My leg's all twisted."

Jessie crawled past him and got to her knees. The rifle fire had stopped, but she could hear men shouting through the trees. Suddenly, a horse blew air and crashed through the brush above.

Jessie jerked up and stared, clawed desperately for the derringer tucked in her belt and brought the weapon up fast. She knew it was too late, too late for anything at all. Barbara wrenched her mount to a stop and leveled the rifle at Jessie's head. Her eyes were as cold as ice, her lips spread in a terrible grin. Jessie waited for the pain that had to come, watched Barbara squeeze the trigger and saw the perfectly sculptured face disappear, the white flesh blossom into a ragged red flower.

Barbara jerked like a rag doll and fell to the ground and lay still. A branch snapped. Jessie turned and stared. Elaina Culbertson stepped into the clearing. She looked at Barbara, dropped the rifle, and started shaking.

Jessie went to her and held her, but Elaina didn't seem to notice she was there . . .

★

Chapter 18

Ki pried dead hands from his throat, rolled away, and came to his feet in a crouch. His eyes searched the rocky terrain, the shadows of the trees. Nothing. An unnatural silence had fallen over the side of the hill. The men who'd been chasing him up the slope had suddenly vanished. Two horses were tied to a tree. Another was running loose.

Scattered gunfire sounded across the valley. Ki stepped carefully into the open and squinted out over the grass. Three riders were making tracks to the south. Another disappeared in the trees to the north. Riding over the valley were a dozen or more men in work shirts and denims. Ki recognized two of them; they were the hands who'd traveled with Elaina from her ranch. But who the hell were the others?

A shout went up behind him. Ki heard his name and looked up. He breathed a sigh of relief as Jessie walked out of the trees and waved both hands over her head. Marcus was beside her. He had his arms over two riders' shoulders and they were helping him down the slope. Ki waved back and turned to the horses tied nearby. Jessie was all right. Now he could do what had to be done.

He left his horse in the courtyard and walked up the steps into the tower. For a moment he stopped and listened, holding one of the dead men's pistols in his hand. Nothing. No sound at all. He walked into the big dining hall. Sunlight traced a bright yellow bar across the floor and the long table. The table was set with white linen and china for a lunch that no one would eat.

Crossing the room, he peered into the kitchen. Something syrupy and sweet had spilled on the floor, and two rangy cats were lapping it up. A kettle had boiled dry on the stove; the smell of burned food was in the air. Ki wondered where all the help were hiding.

Moving back through the dining room, he found the stairs to the second level, and from there up to the third. He turned the wrong way, walked back, and found a corridor that looked familiar. The door was closed but not locked. Inside was Dr. Sacchetti's desk, and there was another door at the end of the room. Ki stood before it for a moment, then pushed it slowly aside. The stone bridge was as he remembered it, and the courtyard below, and the high wall that separated one world from another. He let his eyes trace every inch of the tower, the long, shaded porch, the narrow windows cut in stone.

He knew Aurochs was there . . .

Another man might run, but Aurochs would not. He would come here, and he would wait. It was a thing Ki understood, for long ago he had chosen a code to live by, a path he'd willed himself to follow. Aurochs had a path of his own—a darker, more terrible way. His code was a code of death. He was a killer, and he had been cheated of his kill—and he was as faithful to his path as Ki was to his.

If he'd meet me alone it wouldn't matter . . . even if I have to go down with him . . .

He knew, though, that wasn't Aurochs' way.

He smelled the air, sent his senses across the bridge, felt every tendon in his body come alive. Crouching low, he darted through the door into the open. The sound came at once, scarcely more than a whisper. He wrenched himself aside, and felt the

168

razored edge of the bolt whisper past his cheek. It struck stone, and before it clattered to a stop he was safely across the bridge.

Ki leaned against the wall and breathed slowly. The weapon was a crossbow. It had been fired from high above, which meant that Aurochs had waited patiently behind one of the narrow windows of the tower, knowing Ki would come. If he used the weapon again, it would take a moment to load. When they faced each other, Aurochs could only use it once.

Ki padded around the tower, under the vaulted ceiling of the porch. There was a door, and a stairway leading upstairs. It was a death trap, of course. Aurochs could almost take a nap and still kill him as he poked his head out the top.

He leaned over the porch and looked up. There were footholds between the stones, and he could climb the outside wall. Only there was no place to go after that. Narrow slit windows and nothing more.

Aurochs knows that too. The stairs are the only way to him. He knows that and he's waiting ...

He drew the pistol from the waist of his denims and checked the chamber, then quietly thumbed back the hammer. The stairs circled the inside of the tower. A dusty beam of light touched the wall. He took a careful step, and then another. He stopped and listened. Aurochs was up there for certain; Ki could smell him, the sweat of his body, the odor of his fear. That, and something worse, something that wasn't Aurochs at all ...

"Stop—you no come higher!" Aurochs' bellow echoed down the stairs, and Ki froze.

"Let the girl go," Ki said flatly. "This is our fight not hers."

Aurochs laughed, a sound that chilled Ki's blood. "You throw up pistol. Throw up here and we talk."

Ki cursed under his breath. That was bad luck. The son of a bitch had spotted the gun when he crossed the bridge.

"Let her go. Let her come down here, and you can have the pistol."

Aurochs chuckled. "No," he said, "I have better way. You listen. Girl, sing for man. Sing for him good!"

Ki clenched his fists and shut his eyes. The sound that came from above made his blood run cold. It was the desperate, pitiful cry of an animal, a noise from a mouth and lips that didn't work, a throat that had no more human sounds left ...

"Goddamn you!" he raged. "Stop it, *stop it!*"

The awful sound died. Aurochs laughed. "You don't like song, I make 'er do somet'ing else . . ."

"All right. I'm throwing up the gun," Ki said tightly.

"Slow. Do very slow," growled Aurochs.

Ki took three careful steps and tossed the pistol up the steps. Aurochs let it lay.

"Now. *You* come. Real slow."

"Why? So you can kill me with that thing?"

Aurochs sighed. "You are good fighter. I do not think you foolish man. You come and I kill you, yes? Only maybe I miss, eh? You get chance. You don't come, girl sing some more. I do somet'ing to her an' she sing good. I don't think you like this. I think maybe you come."

Ki took a deep breath. His heart beat rapidly against his chest. Going up there wouldn't help Annie. If he walked up those steps, Aurochs would kill him and it wouldn't do anyone a damn bit of good.

"All right. All right, I'm coming up now."

He climbed the stairs one at a time, knowing the madman's finger might be tightening on the trigger at that moment. Maybe he'd already decided simply to kill him when he stepped in sight. Or maybe he'd wait, draw out the dark joy of the kill.

"Ah, no further—no further!"

Ki stopped. Sun from the high window was in his eyes, and Aurochs stood in the shadow. Only a slice of his face was in the light—flat, ruined features so twisted with fury and pleasure that he seemed more like a demon than a man.

"Where is she?" Ki spat. "What have you done with her?" He squinted into shadow, took a step forward.

"Stop!" The dull gleam of the crossbow swept into the light. Aurochs held it steady in the crook of his arm, a finger on the trigger. "You move, I put this in your gut."

Ki's eyes didn't waver. "I threw up my weapon and I'm here. Now where is she?"

Aurochs laughed. "She not so good for you now, I think."

"Goddamn you!"

Suddenly, Aurochs reached down beside him with his free hand and brought something up from the floor. For a second,

170

Ki didn't know what he was seeing. Then, to his horror, the ruined thing took form.

Ki cried out, staggered back as if Aurochs had struck him. *Annie, Annie!*

He had used her, cut her, hurt her in a hundred different places. Ki didn't know her face because it was hardly a face at all, but he knew her eyes and knew that she could see him . . .

Aurochs beamed with pleasure. "I tell you, yes? She no good for you. Good to Aurochs, though. I think she like Aurochs plenty!"

He squeezed her then, hugged the broken thing to him like a lover. A terrible wail came from Annie's ruined lips.

Ki didn't move. He looked steadily at Aurochs, putting Annie out of his mind. It took every ounce of will, a lifetime of training in *kakuto bugei,* the way of the samurai warrior, but finally it was there. Slowly his feelings faded to nothing, withered like dead winter leaves and disappeared. Now Aurochs alone filled his mind.

"You are afraid of me," he said evenly. "You are afraid to fight me because you know I can kill you. That I am better than you are."

For a moment, Aurochs' pale eyes blazed. Then a terrible smile touched his lips. "You like to trick me, yes? You think I give you the girl."

"You have ruined the girl," Ki said coldly. "I don't want her. She is no use to me. I want you. I want to fight you."

"You want to die, then," sneered Aurochs. "Last time, I beat you plenty bad. You forget this, eh?"

Ki forced a grin. "You are very good at fighting men who can't fight back. And you are good at hurting women. I think they'll remember your name for that. Aurochs, the fighter of women."

Aurochs fought for control. His eyes gleamed with dark, animal cunning. "You talk yourself to death. With this, I kill you like a bug. Snap! You are dead!"

Ki shook his head. "With such a weapon, a child could kill me, Aurochs. You know that as well as I."

From the corner of his eye, Ki saw something that made his flesh crawl. There was a tiny spark of reason in Annie's eyes, a faint touch of purpose that fought through pain to reach

171

out and touch him. Her hand moved up along her thigh, struggled to remember what it could do. It grasped at her belly, inched its way toward her breasts . . .

Ki held his eyes on Aurochs. "You saved me out there because I was your enemy, and you wanted my death for yourself. Is this what you saved me for? So you could kill me with *that?* Put it down. *Fight* me."

"I kill you, is what I do!" growled Aurochs. "Is too much talk!"

"You are not a man," said Ki. "You are afraid. You cannot fight a man."

Aurochs' whole body trembled with rage. The crossbow came up an inch.

"Go on," Ki said tightly. "Do it. Show me what you are!"

Aurochs' finger tightened. Ki could see the pleasure in his eyes, the taste of pain on his lips . . . and at that instant Annie's hand moved, bumping feebly against the big man's wrist . . .

Aurochs bellowed in fury. The steel bow snapped like the crack of a rifle. The deadly bolt kissed the flesh of Ki's shoulder and kept going. Aurochs thrust the empty weapon at Ki, who bobbed aside but kept his footing.

Aurochs tossed Annie aside and came at him. Ki let him come, then moved aside at the final instant and whipped out his heel in a blow aimed at the inguinal plexus of nerves between Aurochs' groin and his thigh. Aurochs howled and went down, the nerves in his leg momentarily deadened. Ki moved in and pounded him mercilessly, slamming his foot again and again into Aurochs' ribs. Finally, Aurochs rolled and came to his feet, at that instant taking a blow from Ki's fist that broke several teeth and brought a gush of blood from between his lips. Aurochs launched a feint with his left fist, then suddenly spun around and leaped for the far side of the room.

Ki saw instantly what he was after. The revolver he'd thrown up the stairs lay hidden in shadow. He leaped in Aurochs' path to cut him off, hit him solidly in the shoulder, and knocked him aside. Aurochs reached out wildly, caught Ki's neck, and turned him around. Ki lost his footing, saw the stairwell looming over his shoulder, flailed out, and wrapped his arms firmly around Aurochs' massive chest. The big man bellowed in surprise. Ki felt his head hit stone, and then they were tumbling down the stairs, locked together. Ki thrust himself away, to let Aurochs land in a heap. Aurochs came up slowly, shaking his head to clear it. Ki hit him hard, his open hands slashing like knives at the bull-like neck. Aurochs choked and backed away. Ki moved in relentlessly. His hands opened Aurochs' cut cheeks further, snapped the bridge of his nose. Ki hit the man again and again, driving him along the shaded porch. Aurochs reeled. His lips hung open; blood from the ruined nose poured into his mouth. Ki slashed at his throat and his eyes. Aurochs held up his hands to ward off the blows, and Ki swept his guard aside. Aurochs staggered, swayed, bent at the waist. Ki stopped, waited a fraction of a second for the man to go down, and saw the gleam in Aurochs' eyes too late . . .

The big fist came up out of nowhere, took Ki full in the jaw, and lifted him off the ground. He hit the stone porch hard, rolled, and felt the darkness close in. He knew that if he didn't get to his feet he was dead.

Aurochs came at him in a blur, caught Ki in a crouch, and kneed him solidly in the head. Ki's neck snapped back. He collapsed on his belly, tried desperately to push himself up. Aurochs' big boot came down for his spine. Ki saw through a haze, and rolled aside as the boot hit stone with a shudder. Aurochs bellowed in rage and kicked Ki solidly in the chest. Ki took the blow in his muscular belly and held on. Aurochs jerked his foot to break free. Ki poured all the strength he had into his legs, came off the ground, and jammed his shoulder in Aurochs' crotch.

Aurochs screamed, flailing his arms for balance. Ki snapped his legs straight and brought the big man up on his shoulder. Aurochs teetered and jerked free. His shoulder slammed hard against the railing of the porch. He balanced there a moment, eyes wide with horror, then his legs went over his shoulders and he was gone . . .

Ki came down the steps of the tower, stopped, and looked at Aurochs. He lay on his back in the courtyard. One arm was twisted under his body. His neck was cocked at an awkward angle. He stared blankly at Ki, his mouth chewing air like a fish. Ki knew everything was broken inside. Aurochs was screaming, but he made no sound. He could die in a minute or last half the day. Or Ki could put a bullet in his head and end it for him now. He looked in the man's eyes, then turned away and walked back toward the tower.

Chapter 19

For a week after the fight west of the mountains, the *Rocky Mountain News* sold all the papers it could print. Every town in the country picked up the stories, and several sent reporters of their own to Denver. Everyone who'd been at the Forsman retreat had something to say. There were personal accounts by Charles and Amanda van Rijn and the other prominent guests. There were interviews with Marshal Billy Vail and members of the Denver police. There was more than one story about the hands at Lane Forsman's ranch who'd saved the day after one of Elaina's riders sounded the alarm. The reporters liked the irony of that: Lane Forsman's own dollar-a-day cowhands had driven off "hordes of foreign black-shirted bullies and thugs," unaware that their boss was raising a bigger money herd up on the hill than they were down in the valley.

The "harem of cunning and treacherous beauties" was worth a story every day—especially after Billy Vail's deputy marshals found the whole bunch lost and hungry, wandering out in the hills near Illinois Creek, northwest of the retreat. Deputy

U.S. Marshal Cal Higgins was quoted all over the country, and in most of the foreign press:

"They was about twenty-five of 'em," said Higgins, "all dressed up like a pack of nuns. Only I seen a couple of nuns once in Taos, and didn't either of them look at me like these gals did!"

Marcus Hall, whom the press had branded a "scandalous rake" a few days before, was now hailed as "the hero of the Rockies, a brave, corruption-fighting senator who should go far in the service of his country."

Jessie Starbuck granted several interviews, and was not particularly surprised to note, when she read them later, that all mention of the cartel and its activities had been deleted. In fact, the story itself was so sensational that no one seemed especially interested in the reasons behind the Forsmans' activities. Jessie accepted it all with resignation born of years of struggle against the cartel and its minions. It appeared as though the fight would be hers and Ki's alone for a while longer . . .

Elaina Culbertson, called "one of the true heroines of our time," was in seclusion at her ranch, recovering from her experiences.

Lawmen in every state and territory soon had ex-Senator Lane Forsman's picture on a poster, but no one was spending any time trying to find him. If he didn't die in the wilds, he'd turn up sooner or later and get caught, and there was no way now that he could cause anyone much trouble . . .

Four days after the fight, Marcus was on his feet with a cane, complaining about limping around doing nothing when he was sorely needed back in Washington. Jessie spent the morning with him, then walked to the stables and got a horse and rode out of town. Half an hour later she crossed the dry creek and climbed the bluff and saw Ki sitting in the shadow of a pinyon. His mount grazed nearby, and his blanket and cooking gear lay just beyond the tree. He looked up and smiled, and Jessie slid off her horse and joined him.

"Well, you're looking better," she said.

"My body is healed. I have my strength back again."

"Good. Only I wasn't really asking about your body."

176

Ki looked at his hands. "The other is a thing that takes longer. Sitting out here has helped."

"Uh-huh." Jessie faced him, her green eyes narrowed with determination. "I know this is something you don't want to talk about, but I figure I've got special privileges, and I intend to use them or abuse them right now. Don't you think you're being a little hard on yourself?"

"Do you think it is something I should forget?"

"No, I sure don't. I can't imagine you doing that. Ki, listen—" Her voice was softer, gentler now. "You did what you did because you cared for her. There wasn't anything else you could do."

Ki shook his head. "She might have been helped. Maybe she would have gotten better."

"Now you know better than that, and so do I." Jessie came to him and held his face between her hands. "I don't guess it's ever occurred to you that it took a lot more courage to do what you did for Annie than it would to have done nothing at all."

"No. I don't think I can let it go like that."

Jessie sighed and lightly cuffed the side of his head. "You samurais have got an answer for everything. Wouldn't hurt, though, if you threw in a little Texas common sense now and then. You think about that." She stood abruptly and brushed off her denims. "Anyway, we've got some business to finish up. I figure we've waited long enough."

Ki's eyes rose to meet hers. "Yes. Long enough, Jessie."

"In the morning, if it's all right with you. You want to ride back with me or meet me later?"

"I don't know if I am yet a fit companion."

"Bullshit," Jessie said bluntly, and grinned at his expression. "Come on, I'll take an *unfit* companion if I can't get anything else. Oh, yes—Amanda was asking for you again. I told her you weren't worth talking to at the moment, but I still had hopes."

Ki looked solemn. "If she is asking about me, I suppose I should see her."

"Uh-huh. Well I wouldn't until I was *fit*. Not Amanda van Rijn." She looked away and studied the sky, but not before she caught the pink flush rise to his face . . .

177

She rode to the Culbertson ranch after breakfast, left her mount with one of the hands, and was ushered inside. Elaina Culbertson sat in the half-darkened parlor, in the same heavy chair Jessie remembered from before. She was pale, her flesh drawn like parchment over her face, but her eyes were bright and dark and full of life. She smiled as Jessie entered and squeezed her hand.

"It was lovely of you to come," she said warmly. "A very pleasant surprise, Jessica."

Jessie sat back in her chair. "Ki and I are taking the Denver & Rio Grande tomorrow at noon. There are some things I wanted to talk to you about before we left."

"I'm most pleased you did," said Elaina.

"Something's kind of bothered me about all this business from the start. I guess it hit Ki the same way, and Marcus too. Only we didn't have time to think much about it till it was over."

"Well, no, I don't imagine so. None of us had much time to think, did we?"

"There were just too many questions, too many things that didn't fit. I've run into the cartel before, Mrs. Culbertson. I'm getting to know them pretty well, and they just don't make a whole lot of mistakes. It bothered me a lot when Barbara asked us up to her place, and then pulled that stunt with the horses. Marcus and I talked about it then. Barbara would be crazy to try to do us in on that trip. Billy Vail knew how we felt about the Forsmans, and they had no idea who else I might have told. Suspicion would fall right in their laps if something happened. Especially with some of Denver's most prominent citizens right close by."

Elaina shook her head and sighed. "I wasn't quite as surprised as you were, Jessica. You must remember, I knew Barbara only too well. She was an extremely cunning woman, but very brazen and erratic at times. Particularly near the end. I really don't think she thought anyone could stand in her way."

"I know," said Jessie, "but it still doesn't make much sense. Whatever Barbara Forsman might have been, the cartel is just not that careless. And they keep a very firm hold on the people who work for them. No, after I had some time to think, the only thing I could figure out was that someone else was running the show—not Barbara. Someone who was deliberately running Barbara down the wrong path."

Jessie stopped and looked at the sun-filled patio past Elaina. "There was only one reason I could see for doing a thing like that," she went on. "Whoever was really behind the cartel's operation knew the cat was out of the bag right from the start. They knew, because they got it out of Lynnie before they killed her. They knew Lynnie had sent me the note—and worse than that, the torn bit of handerkerchief with the cartel's symbol. They certainly knew who *I* was, because they'd tangled with me before. They knew I'd recognize the symbol at once and know the cartel was involved. Right then, I think, this person began to plan for the worst. What if things went wrong? What if I learned something that could link the cartel to the operation? So the person who knew I'd seen the symbol decided *not* to tell Barbara—in case the time came when Barbara would have to be thrown to the wolves."

"Why would this . . . person do that?" asked Elaina. "Wouldn't it be simpler just to kill you, get you out of the picture?"

"Oh, sure. And they *did* try. Only before they could do me in, I'd learned too much, talked to too many people about Lynnie's links with the Forsmans. There was only one thing to do that made sense—be ready to sacrifice the operation, and Barbara along with it. Make it look like the business at the retreat was all there was. Only I'm almost certain that's not true. I know the cartel, and that isn't the way they work. I'd be willing to bet there are a couple of other centers somewhere, training young women for higher places."

Jessie paused, then went on, "I don't think Lane was ever a part of it. You told me that, and you were right. He knew what was happening, but that's about all. He's weak; the cartel would never trust him. Barbara ran the show, at least on the surface. With Dr. Sacchetti's help. But *you* were behind Barbara, weren't you, Mrs. Culbertson? The poor, terrified victim, scared to death of Barbara Forsman. It was a marvelous act, and I believed it. The minute you knew I'd tied in Barbara with Lynnie, you pointed me toward Barbara's involvement with every chance you got."

Jessie shook her head and leaned forward. "Barbara didn't use you; it was the other way around. She was smart, but she was no match for Elaina Culbertson. She did exactly as she was told, right to the end."

"Good Lord, Jessica!" Elaina's eyes went wide. "You can't be serious about this. How can you imagine that I—"

"That a lovely person like Elaina Culbertson could be behind such an operation? It's getting easier all the time."

"Nonsense!" Elaina's hand trembled on her cane. "You—you've gone completely out of your mind!"

"No, I think I'm making sense for the first time since this business started. My coming to your room that night was just about perfect, wasn't it? If I hadn't figured some way for us to talk, you'd have come up with it yourself. You were just playing it by ear, letting things happen. That business of having me execute Ki must really have appealed to Barbara. She'd like something like that. And you kept feeding her ego, telling her how clever she was, that she could never get caught. I don't know what you told her you had in the works for Marcus and me, but I'm sure it was something that would backfire and show up Barbara for what she was. When Aurochs went berserk, though, that was the answer to your prayers. Sacchetti was dead, and all you had to do was get rid of Barbara. They were the only people in the operation who knew what you were. As you'd figured from the start, you might not *have* to get rid of us. If things worked out, we'd be much more useful alive. You'd simply lie low awhile, then take up again right where you left off. And no one would ever be the wiser."

Elaina's dark eyes flashed. A taut smile creased the corners of her mouth. "Very good, Jessica. You have most all of it right. There's only one problem, my dear. Proof. You don't have it, and you won't find any, you know. Even if Lane Forsman is eventually found, do you think he would corroborate your story? He's a coward. He would take some of the blame, and place the rest on Barbara. As you know very well, the real minds behind this wonderful plan do not take betrayal kindly."

She sighed deeply and shook her head. "No, my dear. Your only hope is to extract a confession from me, in front of the proper authorities."

180

"That is what Jessie and I had in mind, Mrs. Culbertson," said Ki, stepping out from behind the draperies over the window through which he had silently entered the room.

Elaina didn't even turn around, but kept her eyes fixed on Jessie's. A small smile curled her lips at the corners. "My masters have been good to me," she said. "They provided me with a means of escape, should this eventuality arise."

"I'm afraid there's no escape, Mrs. Culbertson," Jessie said.

"Oh, but my dear, I already have escaped," the old woman said. Opening a gloved hand, she extended it toward Jessie. In her palm was a small blue glass bottle, empty. "When your arrival was announced, I knew it was time."

She sat back in her chair. A slight tremor passed through her body, and her head lolled back. The hand holding the bottle fell to her lap, and the bottle rolled onto the floor.

Ki walked around from behind the woman's chair and stood with Jessie, who finally bent down and picked up the bottle. Straightening again, she faced Ki and said, "I think you should leave now. Go back the way you came. Do you think you can get out without being seen?"

Ki smiled, and Jessie said, "Silly question, I guess. I'll have to go see Billy Vail. There are bound to be questions. Then I'll see you at the Windsor." She sighed deeply. "It never ends, does it, Ki? And there are never any easy solutions."

Ki reached out a hand and touched her cheek gently. "Maybe someday, Jessie . . ."

She nodded slowly. "Maybe."

Watch for

LONE STAR
AND THE RAILROAD WAR

fourteenth in the hot new
LONE STAR series from Jove

coming in September!

The hottest trio
in Western history
is riding your way
in these giant
LONGARM
adventures!

The matchless lawman LONGARM teams up with the
fabulous duo Jessie and Ki of LONE STAR fame for
exciting Western tales that are not to be missed!

_____ 07386-5   LONGARM AND THE
                LONE STAR LEGEND $2.95
_____ 07085-8   LONGARM AND THE
                LONE STAR VENGEANCE $2.95